Prairie Folks

Prairie Folks

By

HAMLIN GARLAND

Author of

Main-Travelled Roads
Rose of Dutcher's Coolly
The Trail of the Goldseekers
Boy Life on the Prairie, etc.

New Edition

Revised and Enlarged

AMS PRESS
NEW YORK

Reprinted from the edition of 1899, New York
First AMS EDITION published 1969
Manufactured in the United States of America

Library of Congress Catalogue Card Number: 76-98403

AMS PRESS, INC.
New York, N.Y. 10003

PRAIRIE FOLKS

PIONEERS

They rise to mastery of wind and snow;
  They go like soldiers grimly into strife,
To colonize the plain; they plough and sow,
  And fertilize the sod with their own life
As did the Indian and the buffalo.

SETTLERS

Above them soars a dazzling sky,
  In winter blue and clear as steel,
In summer like an arctic sea
  Wherein vast icebergs drift and reel
And melt like sudden sorcery.

Beneath them plains stretch far and fair,
  Rich with sunlight and with rain;
Vast harvests ripen with their care
  And fill with overplus of grain
Their square, great bins.

Yet still they strive! I see them rise
  At dawn-light, going forth to toil:
The same salt sweat has filled my eyes,
  My feet have trod the self-same soil
Behind the snarling plough.

Preface

THE stories which make up PRAIRIE FOLKS were written at about the same time with those contained in " Main-Travelled Roads," and the volume may be considered a companion piece or second series. In the first volume some stories not of the prairie country were included, and the plan of the book brought together stories peculiarly sombre in effect; in " Prairie Folks " the tales are nearly all of the prairie lands of the West, and include many ruder as well as younger types. Both books refer to conditions that have already passed or are passing away. Some of them refer to border life of twenty or thirty years ago, others are of more recent date; all are descriptive of life as I saw it, and are written without regard to any other point of view.

HAMLIN GARLAND.

WEST SALEM, WIS.,
August 16, 1899.

Contents

WILLIAM BACON'S MAN

THEN IT'S SPRING

WHEN the hens begin a-squawkin'
  An' a-rollin' in the dust;
When the rooster takes to talkin',
  An' a-crowin' fit to bust;
When the crows are cawin', flockin',
  An' the chickuns boom and sing,
    Then it's spring!

When the roads are jest one mud-hole
  And the worter tricklin' round
Makes the barn-yard like a puddle,
  An' softens up the ground
Till y'r ankle-deep in worter,
Sayin' words y'r hadn't orter —
  When the jay-birds swear an' sing,
    Then it's spring!

WILLIAM BACON'S MAN

I

THE yellow March sun lay powerfully on the bare
Iowa prairie, where the ploughed fields were already turning warm and brown, and only here and there in a corner
or on the north side of the fence did the sullen drifts
remain, and they were so dark and low that they hardly
appeared to break the mellow brown of the fields.

There passed also an occasional flock of geese, cheerful harbingers of spring, and the prairie-chickens had
set up their morning symphony, wide-swelling, wonderful
with its prophecy of the new birth of grass and grain
and the springing life of all breathing things. The crow
passed now and then, uttering his resonant croak, but
the crane had not yet sent forth his bugle note.

Lyman Gilman rested on his axe-helve at the woodpile of Farmer Bacon to listen to the music around him.
In a vague way he was powerfully moved by it. He
heard the hens singing their weird, raucous, monotonous
song, and saw them burrowing in the dry chip-dust near
him. He saw the young colts and cattle frisking in the
sunny space around the straw-stacks, absorbed through
his bare arms and uncovered head the heat of the sun,
and felt the soft wooing of the air so deeply that he
broke into an unwonted exclamation : —

3

"Glory! we'll be seeding by Friday, sure."

This short and disappointing soliloquy was, after all, an expression of deep emotion. To the Western farmer the very word "seeding" is a poem. And these few words, coming from Lyman Gilman, meant more and expressed more than many a large and ambitious spring-time song.

But the glory of all the slumbrous landscape, the stately beauty of the sky with its masses of fleecy vapor, were swept away by the sound of a girl's voice humming, "Come to the Saviour," while she bustled about the kitchen near by. The windows were open. Ah! what suggestion to these dwellers in a rigorous climate was in the first unsealing of the windows! How sweet it was to the pale and weary women after their long imprisonment!

As Lyman sat down on his maple log to hear better, a plump face appeared at the window, and a clear, girl-voice said: —

"Smell anything, Lime?"

He snuffed the air. "Cookies, by the great horn spoons!" he yelled, leaping up. "Bring me some, an' see me eat; it'll do ye good."

"Come an' get 'm," laughed the face at the window.

"Oh, it's nicer out here, Merry Etty. What's the rush? Bring me out some, an' set down on this log."

With a nod Marietta disappeared, and soon came out with a plate of cookies in one hand and a cup of milk in the other.

"Poor little man, he's all tired out, ain't he?"

Lime, taking the cue, collapsed in a heap, and said feebly, " Bread, bread ! "

" Won't milk an' cookies do as well ? "

He brushed off the log and motioned her to sit down beside him, but she hesitated a little and colored a little.

" Oh, Lime, s'pose somebody should see us ? "

" Let 'em. What in thunder do we care ? Sit down an' gimme a holt o' them cakes. I'm just about done up. I couldn't 'a' stood it another minute."

She sat down beside him with a laugh and a pretty blush. She was in her apron, and the sleeves of her dress were rolled to her elbows, displaying the strong, round arms. Wholesome and sweet she looked and smelled, the scent of the cooking round her. Lyman munched a couple of the cookies and gulped a pint of milk before he spoke.

" Whadda we care who sees us sittin' side b' side ? Ain't we goin' t' be married soon ? "

" Oh, them cookies in the oven ! " she shrieked, leaping up and running to the house. She looked back as she reached the kitchen door, however, and smiled with a flushed face. Lime slapped his knee and roared with laughter at his bold stroke.

" Ho ! ho ! " he laughed. " Didn't I do it slick? Ain't nothin' green in *my* eye, I guess." In an intense and pleasurable abstraction he finished the cookies and the milk. Then he yelled : —

" Hey ! Merry — Merry Etty ! "

" Whadda ye want ? " sang the girl from the window, her face still rosy with confusion.

"Come out here and git these things."

The girl shook her head, with a laugh.

"Come out an' git 'm, 'r, by jingo, I'll throw 'em at ye! Come on, now!"

The girl looked at the huge, handsome fellow, the sun falling on his golden hair and beard, and came slowly out to him — came creeping along with her hand outstretched for the plate which Lime, with a laugh in his sunny blue eyes, extended at the full length of his bare arm. The girl made a snatch at it, but his left hand caught her by the wrist, and away went cup and plate as he drew her to him and kissed her in spite of her struggles.

"My! ain't you strong!" she said, half ruefully and half admiringly, as she shrugged her shoulders. "If you'd use a little more o' *that* choppin' wood, Dad wouldn't 'a' lost s' much money by yeh."

Lime grew grave.

"There's the hog in the fence, Merry; what's yer dad goin' t' say — "

"About what?"

"About our gitt'n married this spring."

"I guess you'd better find out what *I'm* a-goin' t' say, Lime Gilman, 'fore you pitch into Dad."

"I *know* what you're a-goin' t' say."

"No, y' don't."

"Yes, but I *do*, though."

"Well, ask me, and see, if you think you're so smart. Jest as like 's not, you'll slip up."

"All right; here goes. Marietty Bacon, ain't you an' Lime Gilman goin' t' be married?"

"No, sir, we ain't," laughed the girl, snatching up the plate and darting away to the house, where she struck up "Weevily Wheat," and went busily on about her cooking. Lime threw a kiss at her, and fell to work on his log with startling energy.

Lyman looked forward to his interview with the old man with as much trepidation as he had ever known, though commonly he had little fear of anything — but a girl.

Marietta was not only the old man's only child, but his housekeeper, his wife having at last succumbed to the ferocious toil of the farm. It was reasonable to suppose, therefore, that he would surrender his claim on the girl reluctantly. Rough as he was, he loved Marietta strongly, and would find it exceedingly hard to get along without her.

Lyman mused on these things as he drove the gleaming axe into the huge maple logs. He was something more than the usual hired man, being a lumberman from the Wisconsin pineries, where he had sold out his interest in a camp not three weeks before the day he began work for Bacon. He had a nice "little wad o' money" when he left the camp and started for La Crosse, but he had been robbed in his hotel the first night in the city, and was left nearly penniless. It was a great blow to him, for, as he said, every cent of that money "stood fer hard knocks an' poor feed. When I smelt of it I could jest see the cold, frosty mornin's and the late nights. I could feel the hot sun on my back like it was when I worked in the harvest-field. By jingo! It kind o' made my toes curl up."

But he went resolutely out to work again, and here he was chopping wood in old man Bacon's yard, thinking busily on the talk which had just passed between Marietta and himself.

"By jingo!" he said all at once, stopping short, with the axe on his shoulder. "If I hadn't 'a' been robbed I wouldn't 'a' come here — I never'd met Merry. Thunder and jimson root! Wasn't that a narrow escape?"

And then he laughed so heartily that the girl looked out of the window again to see what in the world he was doing. He had his hat in his hand and was whacking his thigh with it.

"Lyman Gilman, what in the world ails you to-day? It's perfectly ridiculous the way you yell and talk t' y'rself out there on the chips. You beat the hens, I declare if you don't."

Lime put on his hat and walked up to the window, and, resting his great bare arms on the sill, and his chin on his arms, said: —

"Merry, I'm goin' to tackle 'Dad' this afternoon. He'll be sittin' up the new seeder, and I'm goin' t' climb right on the back of his neck. He's jest *got* t' give me a chance."

Marietta looked sober in sympathy.

"Well! P'raps it's best to have it over with, Lime, but someway I feel kind o' scary about it."

Lime stood for a long time looking in at the window, watching the light-footed girl as she set the table in the middle of the sun-lighted kitchen floor. The kettle hissed, the meat sizzled, sending up a delicious odor; a hen stood in the open door and sang a sort of cheery half-human song, while to and fro moved the sweet-faced, lithe, and powerful girl, followed by the smiling eyes at the window.

" Merry, you look purty as a picture. You look just like the wife I be'n a-huntin' for all these years, sure 's shootin '."

Marietta colored with pleasure.

" Does Dad pay you to stand an' look at me an' say pretty things t' the cook ? "

" No, he don't. But I'm willin' t' do it without pay. I could just stand here till kingdom come an' look at you. Hello! I hear a wagon. I guess I better hump into that woodpile."

" I think so too. Dinner's most ready, and Dad 'll be here soon."

Lime was driving away furiously at a tough elm log when Farmer Bacon drove into the yard with a new seeder in his wagon. Lime whacked away busily while Bacon stabled the team, and in a short time Marietta called, in a long-drawn, musical fashion : —

" Dinner-r-r ! "

After sozzling their faces at the well the two men went in and sat down at the table. Bacon was not much of a talker at any time, and at meal-time, in seeding, eating was the main business in hand; therefore the meal was a silent one, Marietta and Lime not caring to talk on general topics. The hour was an anxious one for her, and an important one for him.

"Wal, now, Lime, seedun' 's the nex' thing," said Bacon, as he shoved back his chair and glared around from under his bushy eyebrows. "We can't do too much this afternoon. That seeder's got t' be set up an' a lot o' seed-wheat cleaned up. You unload the machine while I feed the pigs."

Lime sat still till the old man was heard outside calling "Oo-ee, poo-ee" to the pigs in the yard; then he smiled at Marietta, but she said: —

"He's got on one of his fits, Lime; I don't b'lieve you'd better tackle him t'-day."

"Don't you worry; I'll fix him. Come, now, give me a kiss."

"Why, you great thing! You — took — "

"I know, but I want you to *give* 'em to me. Just walk right up to me an' give me a smack t' bind the bargain."

"I ain't made any bargain," laughed the girl. Then, feeling the force of his tender tone, she added: "Will you behave, and go right off to your work?"

"Jest like a little man — hope t' die!"

"*Lime!*" roared the old man from the barn.

"Hello!" replied Lime, grinning joyously and winking at the girl, as much as to say, "This would paralyze the old man if he saw it."

He went out to the shed where Bacon was at work, as serene as if he had not a fearful task on hand. He was apprehensive that the father might "gig back" unless rightly approached, and so he awaited a good opportunity.

The right moment seemed to present itself along about the middle of the afternoon. Bacon was down on the ground under the machine, tightening some burrs. This was a good chance for two reasons. In the first place, the keen, almost savage eyes were no longer where they could glare on him, and in spite of his cool exterior Lime had just as soon not have the old man looking at him.

Besides, the old farmer had been telling about his "river eighty," which was without a tenant; the man who had taken it, having lost his wife, had grown disheartened and had given it up.

"It's an almighty good chance for a man with a small family. Good house an' barn, good land. A likely young feller with a team an' a woman could do tiptop on that eighty. If he wanted more, I'd let him have an eighty j'inun' —"

"I'd like t' try that m'self," said Lime, as a feeler. The old fellow said nothing in reply for a moment.

"Ef you had a team an' tools an' a woman, I'd jest as lief you'd have it as anybody."

"Sell me your blacks, and I'll pay half down — the balance in the fall. I can pick up some tools, and as for a woman, Merry Etty an' me have talked that over to-day. She's ready to — ready to marry me whenever you say go."

There was an ominous silence under the seeder, as if the father could not believe his ears.

"What's — what's that!" he stuttered. "Who'd you say? What about Merry Etty?"

"She's agreed to marry me."

"The hell you say!" roared Bacon, as the truth burst upon him. "So that's what you do when I go off to town and leave you to chop wood. So you're goun' to git married, hey?"

He was now where Lime could see him, glaring up into his smiling blue eyes. Lime stood his ground.

"Yes, sir. That's the calculation."

"Well, I guess I'll have somethin' t' say about that," said Bacon, nodding his head violently.

"I rather expected y' would. Blaze away. Your privilege — my bad luck. Sail in ol' man. What's y'r objection to me fer a son-in-law?"

"Don't you worry, young feller. I'll come at it soon enough," went on Bacon, as he turned up another burr in a very awkward corner. In his nervous excitement the wrench slipped, banging his knuckle.

"Ouch! Thunder — m-m-m!" howled and snarled the wounded man.

"What's the matter? Bark y'r knuckle?" queried Lime, feeling a mighty impulse to laugh. But when he saw the old savage straighten up and glare at him he sobered. Bacon was now in a frightful temper. The veins in his great, bare, weather-beaten neck swelled dangerously.

"Jest let me say right here that I've had enough o' you. You can't live on the same acre with my girl another day."

"What makes ye think I can't?" It was now the young man's turn to draw himself up, and as he faced the old man, his arms folded and each vast hand grasping an elbow, he looked like a statue of red granite, and the hands resembled the paws of a crouching lion; but his eyes smiled.

"I don't *think*, I know ye won't."

"What's the objection to me?"

"Objection? Hell! What's the inducement? My hired man, an' not three shirts to yer back!"

"That's another; I've got four. Say, old man, did you ever work out for a living?"

"That's none o' your business," growled Bacon a little taken down. "I've worked an' scraped, an' got t'gether a little prop'ty here, an' they ain't no sucker like you goun' to come 'long here, an' live off me, an' spend my prop'ty after I'm dead. You can jest bet high on that."

"Who's goin' t' live on ye?"

"You're aimun' to."

"I ain't, neither."

"Yes, y'are. You've loafed on me ever since I hired ye."

"That's a —" Lime checked himself for Marietta's sake, and the enraged father went on: —

"I hired ye t' cut wood, an' you've gone an' fooled my daughter away from me. Now you just figger up what I owe ye, and git out o' here. Ye can't go too soon t' suit *me*."

Bacon was renowned as the hardest man to handle in Cedar County, and though he was getting old, he was still a terror to his neighbors when roused. He was honest, temperate, and a good neighbor until something carried him off his balance; then he became as cruel as a panther and as savage as a grisly. All this Lime knew, but it did not keep his anger down so much as did the thought of Marietta. His silence infuriated Bacon, who yelled hoarsely: —

" Git out o' this ! "

" Don't be in a rush, ol' man — "

Bacon hurled himself upon Lime, who threw out one hand and stopped him, while he said in a low voice: —

" Stay right where you are, ol' man. I'm dangerous. It's for Merry's sake — "

The infuriated old man struck at him. Lime warded off the blow, and with a sudden wrench and twist threw him to the ground with frightful force. Before Bacon could rise, Marietta, who had witnessed the scene, came flying from the house.

" Lime ! Father ! What are you doing ? "

" I — couldn't help it, Merry. It was him 'r me," said Lime, almost sadly.

" Dad, ain't you got no sense ? What 're you thinking of ? You jest stop right now. I won't have it."

He rose while she clung to him; he seemed a little dazed. It was the first time he had ever been thrown, and he could not but feel a certain respect for his opponent, but he could not give way.

" Pack up yer duds," he snarled, " an' git off'n my land. I'll have the money fer ye when ye come back. I'll give ye jest five minutes to git clear o' here. Merry, you stay here."

The young man saw it was useless to remain, as it would only excite the old man; and so, with a look of apology, not without humor, at Marietta, he went to the house to get his valise. The girl wept silently while the father raged up and down. His mood frightened her.

" I thought ye had more sense than t' take up with such a dirty houn'."

" He ain't a houn'," she blazed forth, " and he's just as good and clean as you are."

" Shut up! Don't let me hear another word out o' your head. I'm boss here yet, I reckon."

Lime came out with his valise in his hand.

" Good-by, Merry," he said cheerily. She started to go to him, but her father's rough grasp held her.

" Set *down*, an' stay there."

Lime was going out of the gate.

" Here! Come and get y'r money," yelled the old man, extending some bills. " Here's twenty — "

" Go to thunder with your money," retorted Lime. " I've had my pay for my month's work." As he said that, he thought of the sunny kitchen and the merry girl, and his throat choked. Good-by to the sweet girl whose smile was so much to him, and to the happy noons and nights her eyes had made for him. He waved his hat at her as he stood in the open gate, and the sun lighted his handsome head into a sort of glory in her eyes. Then he turned and walked rapidly off down the road, not looking back.

The girl, when she could no longer see him, dashed away, and, sobbing violently, entered the house.

II

THERE was just a suspicion of light in the east, a mere hint of a glow, when Lyman walked cautiously around the corner of the house and tapped at Marietta's window. She was sleeping soundly and did not hear, for she had been restless during the first part of the night. He tapped again, and the girl woke without knowing what woke her.

Lyman put the blade of his pocket-knife under the window and raised it a little, and then placed his lips to the crack, and spoke in a sepulchral tone, half groan, half whisper : —

"Merry ! Merry Etty ! "

The dazed girl sat up in bed and listened, while her heart almost stood still.

"Merry, it's me — Lime.   Come to the winder."

The girl hesitated, and Lyman spoke again.

"Come, I hain't got much time.   This is your last chance t' see me.   It's now 'r never."

The girl slipped out of bed, and, wrapping herself in a shawl, crept to the window.

"Boost on that winder," commanded Lyman. She raised it enough to admit his head, which came just above the sill; then she knelt on the floor by the window.

Her eyes stared wide and dark.

"Lime, what in the world do you mean — "

"I mean business," he replied.   "I ain't no last

year's chicken; I know when the old man sleeps the
soundest." He chuckled pleasantly.

" How 'd y' fool old Rove?"

" Never mind about that now; they's something
more important on hand. You've got t' go with
me."

She drew back. " Oh, Lime, I can't!"

He thrust a great arm in and caught her by the
wrist.

" Yes, y' can. This is y'r last chance. If I go off
without ye t'night, I never come back. What makes ye
gig back? Are ye 'fraid o' me?"

" N-no; but — but — "

" But what, Merry Etty?"

" It ain't right to go an' leave Dad all alone. Where
y' goin' t' take me, anyhow?"

" Milt Jennings let me have his horse an' buggy;
they're down the road a piece, an' we'll go right down
to Rock River and be married by sun-up."

The girl still hesitated, her firm, boyish will un-
wontedly befogged. Resolute as she was, she could not
at once accede to his demand.

" Come, make up your mind soon. The old man 'll
fill me with buck-shot if he catches sight o' me." He
drew her arm out of the window and laid his bearded
cheek to it. " Come, little one, we're made for each
other; God knows it. Come! It's him 'r me."

The girl's head dropped, consented.

" That's right! Now a kiss to bind the bargain.
There! What, cryin'? No more o' that, little one.

c

Now I'll give you jest five minutes to git on your Sunday-go-t'-meetin' clo'es. Quick, there goes a rooster. It's gittin' white in the east."

The man turned his back to the window and gazed at the western sky with a wealth of unuttered and unutterable exultation in his heart. Far off a rooster gave a long, clear blast — would it be answered in the barn? Yes; some wakeful ear had caught it, and now the answer came faint, muffled, and drowsy. The dog at his feet whined uneasily as if suspecting something wrong. The wind from the south was full of the wonderful odor of springing grass, warm, brown earth, and oozing sap. Overhead, to the west, the stars were shining in the cloudless sky, dimmed a little in brightness by the faint silvery veil of moisture in the air. The man's soul grew very tender as he stood waiting for his bride. He was rough, illiterate, yet there was something fine about him after all, a kind of simplicity and a gigantic, leonine tenderness.

He heard his sweetheart moving about inside, and mused : " The old man won't hold out when he finds we're married. He can't get along without her. If he does, why, I'll rent a farm here, and we'll go to work housekeepin'. I can git the money. She shan't always be poor," he ended, and the thought was a vow.

The window was raised again, and the girl's voice was heard low and tremulous : —

" Lime, I'm ready, but I wish we didn't — "

He put his arm around her waist and helped her out, and did not put her down till they reached the road.

She was completely dressed, even to her hat and shoes, but she mourned : —

"My hair is every-which-way; Lime, how can I be married so?"

They were nearing the horse and buggy now, and Lime laughed. "Oh, we'll stop at Jennings's and fix up. Milt knows what's up, and has told his mother by this time. So just laugh as jolly as you can."

Soon they were in the buggy, the impatient horse swung into the road at a rattling pace, and as Marietta leaned back in the seat, thinking of what she had done, she cried lamentably, in spite of all the caresses and pleadings of her lover.

But the sun burst up from the plain, the prairie-chickens took up their mighty chorus on the hills, robins met them on the way, flocks of wild geese, honking cheerily, drove far overhead toward the north, and, with these sounds of a golden spring day in her ears, the bride grew cheerful, and laughed.

III

AT about the time the sun was rising, Farmer Bacon, roused from his sleep by the crowing of the chickens on the dry knolls in the fields as well as by those in the barn-yard, rolled out of bed wearily, wondering why he should feel so drowsy. Then he remembered the row with Lime and his subsequent inability to sleep with thinking over it. There was a dull pain in his breast, which made him uncomfortable.

As was his usual custom, he went out into the kitchen and built the fire for Marietta, filled the teakettle with water, and filled the water-bucket in the sink.   Then he went to her bedroom door and knocked with his knuckles as he had done for years in precisely the same fashion.

Rap — rap — rap.   " Hello, Merry!   Time t' git up. Broad daylight, an' birds asingun.' "

Without waiting for an answer he went out to the barn and worked away at his chores.   He took such delight in the glorious morning and the turbulent life of the farmyard that his heart grew light and he hummed a tune which sounded like the merry growl of a lion. " Poo-ee, poo-ee," he called to the pigs as they swarmed across the yard.

" Ahrr! you big, fat rascals, them hams o' yourn is clear money.   One of ye shall go t' buy Merry a new dress," he said as he glanced at the house and saw the smoke pouring out the stovepipe.   " Merry 's a good girl; she's stood by her old pap when other girls 'u'd 'a' gone back on 'im."

While currying horses he went all over the ground of the quarrel yesterday, and he began to see it in a different light.   He began to see that Lyman was a good man and an able man, and that his own course was a foolish one.

" When I git mad," he confessed to himself, " I don't know anythin'.   But I won't give her up.   She ain't old 'nough t' marry yet — and, besides, I need her."

After finishing his chores, as usual, he went to the well and washed his face and hands, then entered the kitchen — to find the tea-kettle boiling over, and no signs of breakfast anywhere, and no sign of the girl.

"Well, I guess she felt sleepy this mornin'. Poor gal! Mebbe she cried half the night."

"Merry!" he called gently, at the door.

"Merry, m' gal! Pap needs his breakfast."

There was no reply, and the old man's face stiffened into a wild surprise. He knocked heavily again and got no reply, and, with a white face and shaking hand, he flung the door open and gazed at the empty bed. His hand dropped to his side; his head turned slowly from the bed to the open window; he rushed forward and looked out on the ground, where he saw the tracks of a man.

He fell heavily into the chair by the bed, while a deep groan broke from his stiff and twitching lips.

"She's left me! She's left me!"

For a long half-hour the iron-muscled old man sat there motionless, hearing not the songs of the hens or the birds far out in the brilliant sunshine. He had lost sight of his farm, his day's work, and felt no hunger for food. He did not doubt that her going was final. He felt that she was gone from him forever. If she ever came back it would not be as his daughter, but as the wife of Gilman. She had deserted him, fled in the night like a thief; his heart began to harden again, and he rose stiffly. His native stubbornness began to assert itself, the first great shock over, and he went out to the kitchen, and prepared, as best he could, a breakfast, and sat down to it. In some way his appetite failed him, and he fell to thinking over his past life, of the death of his wife, and the early death of his only boy. He was still trying to think what his life would be in the future without his girl, when two carriages drove into the yard. It was about the middle of the forenoon, and the prairie-chickens had ceased to boom and squawk; in fact, that was why he knew, for he had been sitting two hours at the table. Before he could rise he heard swift feet and a merry voice and Marietta burst through the door.

"Hello, Pap! How you makin' out with break —"
She saw a look on his face that went to her heart like a knife. She saw a lonely and deserted old man sitting at his cold and cheerless breakfast, and with a remorseful cry she ran across the floor and took him in her arms, kissing him again and again, while Mr. John Jennings and his wife stood in the door.

"Poor ol' Pap! Merry couldn't leave you. She's come back to stay as long as he lives."

The old man remained cold and stern. His deep voice had a relentless note in it as he pushed her away from him, noticing no one else.

"But how do you come back t' me?"

The girl grew rosy, but she stood proudly up.

"I come back the wife of a *man*, Pap; a wife like my mother, an' this t' hang beside hers;" and she laid down a rolled piece of parchment.

"Take it an' go," growled he; "take yer lazy lubber an' git out o' my sight. I raised ye, took keer o' ye when ye was little, sent ye t' school, bought ye dresses, — done everythin' fer ye I could, 'lowin' t' have ye stand by me when I got old, — but no, ye must go back on yer ol' pap, an' go off in the night with a good-f'r-nothin' houn' that nobuddy knows anything about — a feller that never done a thing fer ye in the world — "

" What did you do for mother that she left *her* father and mother and went with you ? How much did you have when you took her away from her good home an' brought her away out here among the wolves an' Indians ? I've heard you an' her say a hundred times that you didn't have a chair in the house. Now, why do you talk so t' me when I want t' git — when Lime comes and asks for me ? "

The old man was staggered. He looked at the smiling face of John Jennings and the tearful eyes of Mrs. Jennings, who had returned with Lyman. But his heart hardened again as he caught sight of Lime looking in at him. His absurd pride would not let him relent. Lime saw it, and stepped forward.

" Ol' man, I want t' take a little inning now. I'm a fair, square man. I asked ye fer Merry as a man should. I told you I'd had hard luck, when I first came here. I had five thousand dollars in clean cash stole from me. I hain't got a thing now except credit, but that's good fer enough t' stock a little farm with. Now, I wan' to be fair and square in this thing. You wan' to rent a farm; I need one. Let me have the river eighty, or I'll take the whole business on a share of a third, an' Merry Etty and I to stay here with you jest as if nothin' 'd happened. Come, now, what d' y' say ?"

There was something winning in the sturdy bearing of the man as he stood before the father, who remained silent and grim.

"Or if you don't do that, why, there's nothin' left fer Merry an' me but to go back to La Crosse, where I can have my choice of a dozen farms. Now this is the way things is standin'. I don't want to be underhanded about this thing — "

"That's a fair offer," said Mr. Jennings in the pause which followed. "You'd better do it, neighbor Bacon. Nobuddy need know how things stood; they were married in my house — I thought that would be best. You can't live without your girl," he went on, "any more 'n I could without my boy. You'd better — "

The figure at the table straightened up. Under his tufted eyebrows his keen gray eyes flashed from one to the other. His hands knotted.

"Go slow!" went on the smooth voice of Jennings, known all the country through as a peacemaker. "Take time t' think it over. Stand out, an' you'll live here alone without chick 'r child; give in, and this house 'll bubble over with noise and young ones. Now is short, and forever's a long time to feel sorry in."

The old man at the table knitted his eyebrows, and a distorted, quivering, ghastly smile broke out on his face. His chest heaved; then he burst forth : —

"Gal, yank them gloves off, an' git me something to eat — breakfus 'r dinner, I don't care which. Lime, you infernal idiot, git out there and gear up them horses. What in thunder you foolun' round about hýere in seed'n'? Come, hustle, all o' ye!"

And they all shouted in laughter, while the old man strode unsteadily but resolutely out toward the barn, followed by the bridegroom, who was still laughing — but silently.

APRIL DAYS

Days of witchery, subtly sweet,
When every hill and tree finds heart,
When winter and spring like lovers meet
In the mist of noon and part —
  In the April days.

Nights when the wood-frogs faintly peep
Once — twice — and then are still,
And the woodpeckers' martial voices sweep
Like bugle notes from hill to hill —
  Through the pulseless haze.

Days when the soil is warm with rain,
And through the wood the shy wind steals,
Rich with the pine and the poplar smell,
And the joyous earth like a dancer reels
  Through April days!

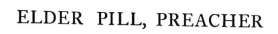

ELDER PILL, PREACHER

ELDER PILL, PREACHER

I

OLD MAN BACON was pinching forked barbs on a wire fence one rainy day in July, when his neighbor Jennings came along the road on his way to town. Jennings never went to town except when it rained too hard to work outdoors, his neighbors said; and of old man Bacon it was said he *never* rested *nights* nor Sundays.

Jennings pulled up. " Good morning, neighbor Bacon."

" Mornin'," rumbled the old man without looking up.

" Taking it easy, as usual, I see. Think it's going to clear up ? "

" May, an' may not. Don't make much differunce t' me," growled Bacon, discouragingly.

" Heard about the plan for a church ? "

" Naw."

" Well, we're goin' to hire Elder Pill from Douglass to come over and preach every Sunday afternoon at the schoolhouse, an' we want help t' pay him — the laborer is worthy of his hire."

" Sometimes he is an' then agin he ain't. Y' needn't look t' me f'r a dollar. I ain't got no intrust in y'r church."

" Oh, yes, you have — besides, y'r sister — "

29

"She ain't got no more time 'n I have t' go t' church. We're obleeged to do 'bout all we c'n stand t' pay our debts, let alone tryun' to support a preacher." And the old man shut the pinchers up on a barb with a vicious grip.

Easy-going Mr. Jennings laughed in his silent way. "I guess you'll help when the time comes," he said, and, clucking to his team, drove off.

"I guess I won't," muttered the grizzled old giant as he went on with his work. Bacon was what is called land poor in the West, that is, he had more land than money; still he was able to give if he felt disposed. It remains to say that he was *not* disposed, being a sceptic and a scoffer. It angered him to have Jennings predict so confidently that he would help.

The sun was striking redly through a rift in the clouds, about three o'clock in the afternoon, when he saw a man coming up the lane, walking on the grass at the side of the road, and whistling merrily. The old man looked at him from under his huge eyebrows with some curiosity. As he drew near, the pedestrian ceased to whistle, and, just as the farmer expected him to pass, he stopped and said, in a free and easy style : —

"How de do? Give me a chaw t'baccer. I'm Pill, the new minister. I take fine-cut when I can get it," he said, as Bacon put his hand into his pocket. "Much obliged. How goes it?"

"Tollable, tollable," said the astounded farmer, looking hard at Pill as he flung a handful of tobacco into his mouth.

" Yes, I'm the new minister sent around here to keep you fellows in the traces and out of hell-fire. Have y' fled from the wrath?" he asked, in a perfunctory way.

" You are, eh?" said Bacon, referring back to his profession.

" I am, just! How do you like that style of barb fence? Ain't the twisted wire better?"

" I s'pose they be, but they cost more."

" Yes, costs more to go to heaven than to hell. You'll think so after I board with you a week. Narrow the road that leads to light, and broad the way that leads — how's your soul anyway, brother?"

" Soul's all right. I find more trouble to keep m' body go'n'."

" Give us your hand; so do I. All the same we must prepare for the next world. We're gettin' old; lay not up your treasures where moth and rust corrupt and thieves break through and steal."

Bacon was thoroughly interested in the preacher, and was studying him carefully. He was tall, straight, and superbly proportioned; broad-shouldered, wide-lunged, and thewed like a Chippewa. His rather small steel-blue eyes twinkled, and his shrewd face and small head, set well back, completed a remarkable figure. He wore his reddish beard in the usual way of Western clergymen, with mustache chopped close.

Bacon spoke slowly : —

" You look like a good, husky man to pitch in the barn-yard; you've too much muscle f'r preachun'."

"Come and hear me next Sunday, and if you say so then, I'll quit," replied Mr. Pill, quietly. "I give ye my word for it. I believe in preachers havin' a little of the flesh and the devil; they can sympathize better with the rest of ye." The sarcasm was lost on Bacon, who continued to look at him. Suddenly he said, as if with an involuntary determination : —

"Where ye go'n' to stay t'night ? "

"I don't know; do you ? " was the quick reply.

"I reckon ye can hang out with me, 'f ye feel like ut. We ain't very purty, at our house, but we eat. You go along down the road and tell 'em I sent yeh. Ye'll find an' ol' dusty Bible round some'rs — I s'pose ye spend y'r spare time read'n' about Joshua an' Dan'l — "

"I spend more time reading men. Well, I'm off! I'm hungrier 'n a gray wolf in a bear-trap." And off he went as he came. But he did not whistle; he chewed.

Bacon felt as if he had made too much of a concession, and had a strong inclination to shout after him, and retract his invitation; but he did not, only worked on, with an occasional bear-like grin. There was something captivating in this fellow's free and easy way.

When he came up to the house an hour or two later, in singular good humor for him, he found the Elder in the creamery, with his niece Eldora, who was not more won by him than was his sister Jane Buttles, he was so genial and put on so few religious frills.

Mrs. Buttles never put on frills of any kind. She was a most frightful toiler, only excelled (if excelled at all)

by her brother. Unlovely at her best, when about her
work in her faded calico gown and flat shoes, hair
wisped into a slovenly knot, she was depressing. But
she was a good woman, of sterling integrity, and ambitious for her girl. She was very glad of the chance to
take charge of her brother's household after Marietta
married.

Eldora was as attractive as her mother was depressing. She was very young at this time and had the physical perfection — at least as regards body — that her
parents must have had in youth. She was above the
average height of woman, with strong swell of bosom
and glorious, erect carriage of head. Her features were
coarse, but regular and pleasing, and her manner boyish.

Elder Pill was on the best terms with them as he
watched the milk being skimmed out of the " submerged
cans " ready for the " caaves and hawgs," as Mrs. Buttles
called them.

" Uncle told you t' come here 'nd stay t' supper, did
he ? What's come over him ? " said the girl, with a
sort of audacious humor.

" Bill has an awful grutch agin preachers," said Mrs.
Buttles, as she wiped her hands on her apron. " I
declare, I don't see how — "

" *Some* preachers, not *all* preachers," laughed Pill, in
his mellow nasal. " There are preachers, and then again
preachers. I'm one o' the t'other kind."

" I sh'd think y' was," laughed the girl.

" Now, Eldory, you run right t' the pig-pen with that
milk, whilst I go in an' set the tea on."

D

Mr. Pill seized the can of milk, saying, with a twang:
"Show me the way that I may walk therein," and,
accompanied by the laughing girl, made rapid way to
the pig-pen just as the old man set up a ferocious shout
to call the hired hand out of the corn-field.

"How'd y' come to send *him* here?" asked Mrs.
Buttles, nodding toward Pill.

"Damfino! I kind o' liked him — no nonsense about
him," answered Bacon, going into temporary eclipse
behind his hands as he washed his face at the cistern.

At the supper table Pill was "easy as an old shoe";
ate with his knife, talked about fatting hogs, suggested a
few points on raising clover, told of pioneer experiences
in Michigan, and soon won them — hired man and all
— to a most favorable opinion of himself. But he did
not trench on religious matters at all.

The hired man in his shirt-sleeves, and smelling
frightfully of tobacco and sweat (as did Bacon), sat with
open mouth, at times forgetting to eat, in his absorbing
interest in the minister's yarns.

"Yes, I've got a family, too much of a family, in
fact — that is, I think so sometimes when I'm pinched.
Our Western people are so indigent — in plain terms,
poor — they *can't* do any better than they do. But we
pull through — we pull through! John, you look like
a stout fellow, but I'll bet a hat I can *down* you three
out of five."

"I bet you can't," grinned the hired man. It was
the climax of all, that bet.

"I'll take y' in hand an' flop y' both," roared Bacon

from his lion-like throat, his eyes glistening with rare good-nature from the shadow of his gray brows. But he admired the minister's broad shoulders at the same time. If this fellow panned out as he promised, he was a rare specimen.

After supper the Elder played a masterly game of croquet with Eldora, beating her with ease; then he wandered out to the barn and talked horses with the hired man, and finished by stripping off his coat and putting on one of Mrs. Buttles's aprons to help milk the cows.

But at breakfast the next morning, when the family were about pitching into their food as usual without ceremony, the visitor spoke in an imperious tone and with lifted hand. "*Wait!* Let us look to the Lord for His blessing."

They waited till the grace was said, but it threw a depressing atmosphere over the group; evidently they considered the trouble begun. At the end of the meal the minister asked : —

"Have you a Bible in the house?"

"I reckon there's one around somewhere. Elly, go 'n see 'f y' can't raise one," said Mrs. Buttles, indifferently.

"Have you any objection to family devotion?" asked Pill, as the book was placed in his hands by the girl.

"No; have all you want," said Bacon, as he rose from the table and passed out the door.

"I guess I'll see the thing through," said the hand.

"It ain't just square to leave the women folks to bear the brunt of it."

It was shortly after breakfast that the Elder concluded he'd walk up to Brother Jennings's and see about church matters.

"I shall expect you, Brother Bacon, to be at the service at 2.30."

"All right, go ahead expectun'," responded Bacon, with an inscrutable sidewise glance.

"You promised, you remember?"

"The — devil — I did!" the old man snarled.

The Elder looked back with a smile, and went off whistling in the warm, bright morning.

II

THE schoolhouse down on the creek was known as "Hell's Corners" all through the county, because of the frequent rows that took place therein at "corkuses" and the like, and also because of the number of teachers that had been "ousted" by the boys. In fact, it was one of those places still to be found occasionally in the West, far from railroads and schools, where the primitive ignorance and ferocity of men still prowl, like the panthers which are also found sometimes in the deeps of the Iowa timber lands.

The most of this ignorance and ferocity, however, was centred in the family of Dixons, a dark-skinned, unsavory group of Missourians. It consisted of old man Dixon and wife, and six sons, all man-grown,

great, gaunt, sinewy fellows, with no education, but
superstitious as savages. If anything went wrong in
" Hell's Corners" everybody knew that the Dixons were
" on the rampage again." The school-teachers were
warned against the Dixons, and the preachers were be-
sought to convert the Dixons.

In fact, John Jennings, as he drove Pill to the schoolhouse next day, said : —

" If you can convert the Dixon boys, Elder, I'll give
you the best horse in my barn."

" I work not for such hire," said Mr. Pill, with a look
of deep solemnity on his face, belied, indeed, by a
twinkle in his small, keen eye — a twinkle which made
Milton Jennings laugh candidly.

There was considerable curiosity, expressed by a murmur of lips and voices, as the minister's tall figure
entered the door and stood for a moment in a study
of the scene before him. It was a characteristically
Western scene. The women sat on one side of the
schoolroom, the men on the other; the front seats
were occupied by squirming boys and girls in their
Sunday splendor.

On the back, to the right, were the young men, in
their best vests, with paper collars and butterfly neck-
ties, with their coats unbuttoned, their hair plastered
down in a fascinating wave on their brown foreheads.
Not a few were in their shirt-sleeves. The older men
sat immediately between the youths and boys, talking in
hoarse whispers across the aisles about the state of the
crops and the county ticket, while the women in mucl

the same way conversed about the children and raising onions and strawberries. It was their main recreation, this Sunday meeting.

"Brethren!" rang out the imperious voice of the minister, "let us pray."

The audience thoroughly enjoyed the Elder's prayer. He was certainly gifted in that direction, and his petition grew genuinely eloquent as his desires embraced the "ends of the earth and the utterm'st parts of the seas thereof." But in the midst of it a clatter was heard, and five or six strapping fellows filed in with loud thumpings of their brogans.

Shortly after they had settled themselves with elaborate impudence on the back seat, the singing began. Just as they were singing the last verse, every individual voice wavered and all but died out in astonishment to see William Bacon come in — an unheard-of thing! And with a clean shirt, too! Bacon, to tell the truth, was feeling as much out of place as a cat in a bath-tub, and looked uncomfortable, even shame-faced, as he sidled in, his shapeless hat gripped nervously in both hands; coatless and collarless, his shirt open at his massive throat. The girls tittered, of course, and the boys hammered each other's ribs, moved by the unusual sight. Milton Jennings, sitting beside Bettie Moss, said : —

"Well! may I jump straight up and never come down!"

And Shep Watson said : "May I never see the back o' my neck!" Which pleased Bettie so much that she grew quite purple with efforts to conceal her laughter; she always enjoyed a joke on her father.

But all things have an end, and at last the room became quiet as Mr. Pill began to read the Scripture, wondering a little at the commotion. He suspected that those dark-skinned, grinning fellows on the back seat were the Dixon boys, and knew they were bent on fun. The physique of the minister being carefully studied, the boys began whispering among themselves, and at last, just as the sermon opened, they began to push the line of young men on the long seat over toward the girls' side, squeezing Milton against Bettie. This pleasantry encouraged one of them to whack his neighbor over the head with his soft hat, causing great laughter and disturbance. The preacher stopped. His cool, penetrating voice sounded strangely unclerical as he said : —

"There are some fellows here to-day to have fun with me. If they don't keep quiet, they'll have more fun than they can hold." (At this point a green crab-apple bounded up the aisle.) "I'm not to be bulldozed."

He pulled off his coat and laid it on the table before him, and, amid a wondering silence, took off his cuffs and collar, saying : —

"I can preach the word of the Lord just as well without my coat, and I can throw rowdies out the door a little better in my shirt-sleeves."

Had the Dixon boys been a little shrewder as readers of human character, or if they had known why old William Bacon was there, they would have kept quiet; but

it was not long before they began to push again, and at
last one of them gave a squeak, and a tussle took place.
The preacher was in the midst of a sentence : —

" An evil deed, brethren, is like unto a grain of mus-
tard seed. It is small, but it grows steadily, absorbing
its like from the earth and air, sending out roots and
branches, till at last — "

There was a scuffle and a snicker. Mr. Pill paused,
and gazed intently at Tom Dixon, who was the most
impudent and strongest of the gang; then he moved
slowly down on the astonished young savage. As he
came his eyes seemed to expand like those of an eagle
in battle, steady, remorseless, unwavering, at the same
time that his brows shut down over them — a glance that
hushed every breath. The awed and astonished ruffians
sat as if paralyzed by the unuttered yet terribly ferocious
determination of the preacher's eyes. His right hand
was raised, the other was clenched at his waist. There
was a sort of solemnity in his approach, like a tiger creeping upon a foe.

At last, after what seemed minutes to the silent,
motionless congregation, his raised hand came down
on the shoulder of the leader with the exact, resistless
precision of the tiger's paw, and the ruffian was snatched
from his seat to the floor sprawling. Before he could
rise, the steel-like grip of the roused preacher sent him
halfway to the door, and then out into the dirt of the
road.

Turning, Pill strode down the aisle once more.
The half-risen congregation made way for him, curiously.

When he came within reach of Dick, the fellow struck
savagely out at the preacher, only to have his blow
avoided by a lithe, lightning-swift movement of the
body above the hips (a trained boxer's trick), and to
find himself lying bruised and dazed on the floor.

By this time the other brothers had recovered from
their stupor, and, with wild curses, leaped over the
benches toward the fearless preacher.

But now a new voice was heard in the sudden uproar
— a new but familiar voice. It was the mighty voice
of William Bacon, known far and wide as a terrible
antagonist, a man who had never been whipped. He
was like a wild beast excited to primitive savagery by
the smell of blood.

"Stand *back*, you hell-hounds!" he said, leaping between them and the preacher. "You know me. Lay
another hand on that man an', by the livun' God, you
answer t' me. Back thear!"

Some of the men cheered, most stood irresolute. The
women crowded together, the children began to scream
with terror, while through it all Pill dragged his last
assailant toward the door.

Bacon made his way down to where the Dixons had
halted, undecided what to do. If the preacher had the
air and action of the tiger, Bacon looked the grisly bear
— his eyebrows working up and down, his hands clenched
into frightful bludgeons, his breath rushing through his
hairy nostrils.

"Git out o' hyare," he growled. "You've run things
here jest about long enough. Git out!"

His hands were now on the necks of two of the boys, and he was hustling them toward the door.

"If you want 'o whip the preacher, meet him in the public road — one at a time; he'll take care o' himself. Out with ye," he ended, kicking them out. "Show your faces here agin, an' I'll break ye in two."

The non-combative farmers now began to see the humor of the whole transaction, and began to laugh; but they were cut short by the calm voice of the preacher at his desk : —

"But a *good* deed, brethren, is like unto a grain of wheat planted in good earth, that bringeth forth fruit in due season an hundred fold."

III

MR. PILL, with all his seeming levity, was a powerful hand at revivals, as was developed at the " protracted " meetings at the Grove during December. Indeed, such was the pitiless intensity of his zeal that a gloom was cast over the whole township; the ordinary festivities stopped or did not begin at all.

The lyceum, which usually began by the first week in December, was put entirely out of the question, as were the spelling-schools and " exhibitions." The boys, it is true, still drove the girls to meeting in the usual manner; but they all wore a furtive, uneasy air, and their laughter was not quite genuine at its best, and died away altogether when they came near the school-house, and they hardly recovered from the effects of the preaching till a mile or two had been spun behind the shining runners. It took all the magic of the jingle of the bells and the musical creak of the polished steel on the snow to win them back to laughter.

As for Elder Pill, he was as a man transformed. He grew more intense each night, and strode back and forth behind his desk and pounded the Bible like an assassin. No more games with the boys, no more poking the girls under the chin! When he asked for a chew of tobacco now it was with an air which said: "I ask it as sustenance that will give me strength for the Lord's service," as if the demands of the flesh had weakened the spirit.

Old man Bacon overtook Milton Jennings early one Monday morning, as Milton was marching down toward the Seminary at Rock River. It was intensely cold and still, so cold and still that the ring of the cold steel of the heavy sleigh, the snort of the horses, and the old man's voice came with astonishing distinctness to the ears of the hurrying youth, and it seemed a very long time before the old man came up.

"Climb on!" he yelled, out of his frosty beard. He was seated on the "hind bob" of a wood-sleigh, on a couple of blankets. Milton clambered on, knowing well he'd freeze to death there.

"Reckon I heerd you prowlun' around the front door with my girl last night," Bacon said at length. "The way you both 'tend out t' meetun' ought 'o sanctify yeh; must 'a' stayed to the after-meetun', didn't yeh?"

"Nope. The front part was enough for —"

" Danged if I was any more fooled with a man in m'
life.   I b'lieve the whole thing is a little scheme on the
bretheren t' raise a dollar."

" Why so ? "

" Waal, y' see, Pill ain't got much out o' the app'int-
ment thus fur, and he ain't likely to, if he don't shake
'em up a leetle.   Borrud ten dollars o' me t'other day."

Well, thought Milton, whatever his real motive is,
Elder Pill is earning all he gets.   Standing for two or
three hours in his place night after night, arguing, pleading, even commanding them to be saved.

Milton was describing the scenes of the meeting to
Bradley Talcott and Douglas Radbourn the next day,
and Radbourn, a young law student, said : —

" I'd like to see him.   He must be a character."

" Let's make up a party and go out," said Milton,
eagerly.

" All right ; I'll speak to Lily Graham."

Accordingly, that evening a party of students, in a
large sleigh, drove out toward the schoolhouse, along
the drifted lanes and through the beautiful aisles of the
snowy woods.   A merry party of young people, who
had no sense of sin to weigh them down.   Even Radbourn and Lily joined in the songs which they sang to
the swift clanging of the bells, until the lights of the
schoolhouse burned redly through the frosty air.

Not a few of the older people present felt scandalized
by the singing and by the dancing of the " town girls,"
who could not for the life of them take the thing seri-
ously.   The room was so little, and hot, and smoky,

and the men looked so queer in their rough coats and hair every-which-way.

But they took their seats demurely on the back seat, and joined in the opening songs, and listened to the halting prayers of the brethren and the sonorous prayers of the Elder, with commendable gravity. Miss Graham was a devout Congregationalist, and hushed the others into gravity when their eyes began to dance dangerously.

However, as Mr. Pill warmed to his work, the girls grew sober enough. He awed them, and frightened them with the savagery of his voice and manner. His small gray eyes were like daggers unsheathed, and his small, round head took on a cat-like ferocity, as he strode to and fro, hurling out his warnings and commands in a hoarse howl that terrified the sinner, and drew " amens " of admiration from the saints.

" Atavism; he has gone back to the era of the medicine man," Radbourn murmured.

As the speaker went on, foam came upon his thin lips; his lifted hand had prophecy and threatening in it. His eyes reflected flames; his voice had now the tone of the implacable, vindictive judge. He gloated on the pictures that his words called up. By the power of his imagination the walls widened, the floor was no longer felt, the crowded room grew still as death, every eye fixed on the speaker's face.

" I tell you, you must repent or die. I can see the great judgment angel now ! " he said, stopping suddenly and pointing above the stovepipe. " I can see him as he stands weighing your souls as a man 'ud weigh wheat

and chaff. Wheat goes into the Father's garner; chaff
is blown to hell's devouring flame! I can see him *now!*
He seizes a poor, damned, struggling soul by the *neck*,
he holds him over the flaming forge of *hell* till his bones
melt like wax; he shrivels like thread in the flame of
a candle; he is nothing but a charred husk, and the
angel flings him back into *outer darkness;* life was not in
him."

It was this astonishing figure, powerfully acted, that
scared poor Tom Dixon into crying out for mercy.
The effect upon others was painful. To see so great a
sinner fall terror-stricken seemed like a providential
stroke of confirmatory evidence, and nearly a dozen
other young people fell crying, whereat the old people
burst out into amens of spasmodic fervor, while the
preacher, the wild light still in his eyes, tore up and
down, crying above the tumult: —

"The Lord is come with *power!* His hand is visible
here. Shout *aloud* and spare *not.* Fall before him as
dust to his feet! Hypocrites, vipers, scoffers! the *lash*
o' the *Lord* is on ye!"

In the intense pause which followed as he waited
with expectant, uplifted face — a pause so deep even
the sobbing sinners held their breath — a dry, drawl-
ing, utterly matter-of-fact voice broke the intense
hush.

"S-a-y, Pill, ain't you a-bearun' down on the boys a
leetle too hard?"

The preacher's extended arm fell as if life had gone
out of it. His face flushed and paled; the people

laughed hysterically, some of them with the tears of terror still on their cheeks; but Radbourn said, " Bravo, Bacon ! "

Pill recovered himself.

" Not hard enough for *you*, neighbor Bacon."

Bacon rose, retaining the same dry, prosaic tone : —

" I ain't bitin' that kind of a hook, an' I ain't goin' to be *yanked* into heaven when I c'n *slide* into hell. Waal ! I must be goin'; I've got a new-milk's cow that needs tendin' to."

The effect of all this was very great. From being at the very mouth of the furnace, quivering with fear and captive to morbid imaginings, Bacon's dry intonation brought them all back to earth again. They perceived something of the absurdity of the whole situation.

Pill was beaten for the first time in his life. He had been struck below the belt by a good-natured giant. The best he could do, as Bacon shuffled calmly out, was to stammer: " Will some one please sing? " And while they sang, he stood in deep thought. Just as the last verse was quivering into silence, the full, deep tones of Radbourn's voice rose above the bustle of feet and clatter of seats : —

" And all *that* he preaches in the name of Him who came bringing peace and good-will to men."

Radbourn's tone had in it reproach and a noble suggestion. The people looked at him curiously. The deacons nodded their heads together in counsel, and when they turned to the desk Pill was gone !

" Gee whittaker ! That was tough," said Milton to

Radbourn; "knocked the wind out o' him like a cannon-ball. What'll he do now?"

"He can't do anything but acknowledge his foolishness."

"You no business t' come here an' 'sturb the Lord's meetin'," cried old Daddy Brown to Radbourn. "You're a sinner and a scoffer."

"I thought Bacon was the disturbing ele —"

"You're just as bad!"

"He's all *right*," said William Councill. "I've got sick, m'self, of bein' *scared* into religion. I never was so fooled in a man in my life. If I'd tell you what Pill said to me the other day, when we was in Robie's store, you'd fall in a fit. An' to hear him talkin' here t'night, is enough to make a horse laugh."

"You're all in league with the devil," said the old man, wildly; and so the battle raged on.

Milton and Radbourn escaped from it, and got out into the clear, cold, untainted night.

"The heat of the furnace doesn't reach as far as the horses," Radbourn moralized, as he aided in unhitching the shivering team. "In the vast, calm spaces of the stars, among the animals, such scenes as we have just seen are impossible." He lifted his hand in a lofty gesture. The light fell on his pale face and dark eyes. The girls were a little indignant and disposed to take the preacher's part. They thought Bacon had no right to speak out that way, and Miss Graham uttered her protest, as they whirled away on the homeward ride with pleasant jangle of bells.

"But the secret of it all was," said Radbourn in answer, "Pill knew he was acting a part. I don't mean that he meant to deceive, but he got excited, and his audience responded as an audience does to an actor of the first class, and he was for the time in earnest; his imagination *did* see those horrors, — he was swept away by his own words. But when Bacon spoke, his dry tone and homely words brought everybody, preacher and all, back to the earth with a thump! Everybody saw, that after weeping and wailing there for an hour, they'd go home, feed the calves, hang up the lantern, put out the cat, wind the clock, and go to bed. In other words, they all came back out of their barbaric *powwow* to their natural modern selves."

This explanation had palpable truth, but Lily perceived that it had wider application than to the meeting they had just left.

"They'll be music around this clearing to-morrow," said Milton, with a sigh; "wish I was at home this week."

"But what'll become of Mr. Pill?"

"Oh, he'll come out all right," Radbourn assured her, and Milton's clear tenor rang out as he drew Eileen closer to his side: —

> "O silver moon, O silver moon,
> You set, you set too soon —
> The morrow day is far away,
> The night is but begun."

E

IV

THE news, grotesquely exaggerated, flew about the next day, and at night, though it was very cold and windy, the house was jammed to suffocation. On these lonely prairies life is so devoid of anything but work, dramatic entertainments are so few, and appetite so keen, that a temperature of twenty degrees below zero is no bar to a trip of ten miles. The protracted meeting was the only recreation for many of them. The gossip before and after service was a delight not to be lost, and this last sensation was dramatic enough to bring out old men and women who had not dared to go to church in winter for ten years.

Long before seven o'clock, the schoolhouse blazed with light and buzzed with curious speech. Team after team drove up to the door, and as the drivers leaped out to receive the women, they said in low but eager tones to the bystanders: —

"Meeting begun yet?"

"Nope!"

"What kind of a time y' havin' over here, any way?"

"A mighty solumn time," somebody would reply with a low laugh.

By seven o'clock every inch of space was occupied; the air was frightful. The kerosene lamps gave off gas and smoke, the huge stove roared itself into an angry red on its jack-oak grubs, and still people crowded in at the door.

Discussion waxed hot as the stove; two or three Universalists boldly attacked everybody who came their way. A tall man stood on a bench in the corner, and, thumping his Bible wildly with his fist, exclaimed, at the top of his voice: —

" There is *no* hell at *all!* The Bible says the *wicked* perish *utterly.* They are *consumed* as *ashes* when they die. They *perish* as *dogs!* "

" What kind o' docterin' is that ? " asked a short man of Councill.

" I d'know. It's ol' Sam Richards. Calls himself a Christian — Christadelphian 'r some new-fangled name."

At last people began to inquire, " Well, ain't he comin' ? "

" Most time f'r the Elder to come, ain't it ? "

" Oh, I guess he's preparin' a sermon."

John Jennings pushed anxiously to Daddy Brown.

" Ain't the Elder comin' ? "

" I d'know. He didn't stay at my house."

" He didn't ? "

" No. Thought he went home with you."

" I ain't see 'im 't all. I'll ask Councill. Brother Councill, seen anything of the Elder ? "

" No. Didn't he go home with Bensen ? "

" I d'n know. I'll see."

This was enough to start the news that " Pill had skipped."

This the deacons denied, saying " he'd come or send word."

Outside, on the leeward side of the house, the young men who couldn't get in stood restlessly, now dancing a jig, now kicking their huge boots against the underpinning to warm their toes. They talked spasmodically as they swung their arms about their chests, speaking from behind their huge buffalo-coat collars.

The wind roared through the creaking oaks; the horses stirred complainingly, the bells on their backs crying out querulously; the heads of the fortunates inside were shadowed outside on the snow, and the restless young men amused themselves betting on which head was Bensen and which Councill.

At last some one pounded on the desk inside. The suffocating but lively crowd turned with painful adjustment toward the desk, from whence Deacon Bensen's high, smooth voice sounded : —

" Brethren an' sisters, Elder Pill hain't come — and, as it's about eight o'clock, he probably won't come tonight. After the disturbances last night, it's — a — a — we're all the more determined to — the — a — need of reforming grace is more felt than ever. Let us hope nothing has happened to the Elder. I'll go see tomorrow, and if he is unable to come — I'll see Brother Wheat, of Cresco. After prayer by Brother Jennings, we will adjourn till to-morrow night. Brother Jennings, will you lead us in prayer ? " (Some one snickered.) " I hope the disgraceful — a — scenes of last night will not be repeated."

" Where's Pill?" demanded a voice in the back part
of the room. " That's what I want to know."

" He's a bad pill," said another, repeating a pun
already old.

" I guess so! He borrowed twenty dollars o' me
last week," said the first voice.

" He owes me for a pig," shouted a short man, ex-
citedly. " I believe he's skipped to get rid o' his
debts."

" So do I. I allus said he was a mighty queer
preacher."

" He'd bear watchin' was my idee fust time I ever
see him."

" Careful, brethren — *careful*. He may come at any
minute."

" I don't care if he does. I'd bone him f'r pay f'r
that shote, preacher 'r no preacher," said Bartlett, a
little nervously.

High words followed this, and there was prospect of
a fight. The pressure of the crowd, however, was so
great it was well-nigh impossible for two belligerents to
get at each other. The meeting broke up at last, and
the people, chilly, soured, and disappointed at the lack
of developments, went home saying Pill was *scaly ;* no
preacher who chawed terbacker was to be trusted, and
when it was learned that the horse and buggy he drove
he owed Jennings and Bensen for, everybody said,
" He's a fraud."

V

IN the meantime, Andrew Pill was undergoing the most singular and awful mental revolution.

When he leaped blindly into his cutter and gave his horse the rein, he was wild with rage and shame, and a sort of fear. As he sat with bent head, he did not hear the tread of the horse, and did not see the trees glide past. The rabbit leaped away under the shadow of the thick groves of young oaks; the owl, scared from its perch, went fluttering off into the cold, crisp air; but he saw only the contemptuous, quizzical face of old William Bacon — one shaggy eyebrow lifted, a smile showing through his shapeless beard.

He saw the colorless, handsome face of Radbourn, and his look of reproach and note of suggestion — Radbourn, one of the best thinkers in Rock River, and the most generally admired young man in Rock County.

When he saw and heard Bacon, his hurt pride flamed up in wrath, but the calm voice of Radbourn, and the look in his stern, accusing eyes, made his head fall in thought. As he rode, things grew clearer. As a matter of fact, his whole system of religious thought was like the side of a shelving sand-bank — in unstable equilibrium — needing only a touch to send it slipping into a shapeless pile at the river's edge. That touch had been given, and he was now in the midst of the motion of his falling faith. He didn't know how much would stand when the sloughing ended.

Andrew Pill had been a variety of things, a farmer, a dry-goods merchant, and a travelling salesman, but in a revival quite like this of his own, he had been converted and his life changed. He now desired to help his fellow-men to a better life, and willingly went out among the farmers, where pay was small. It was not true, therefore, that he had gone into it because there was little work and good pay. He was really an able man, and would have been a success in almost anything he undertook; but his reading and thought, his easy intercourse with men like Bacon and Radbourn, had long since undermined any real faith in the current doctrine of retribution, and to-night, as he rode into the night, he was feeling it all and suffering it all, forced to acknowledge at last what had been long moving.

The horse took the wrong road, and plodded along steadily, carrying him away from his .home, but he did not know it for a long time. When at last he looked up and saw the road leading out upon the wide plain between the belts of timber, leading away to Rock River, he gave a sigh of relief He could not meet his wife then; he must have a chance to think.

Over him, the glittering, infinite sky of winter midnight soared, passionless, yet accusing in its calmness, sweetness, and majesty. What was he that he could dogmatize on eternal life and the will of the Being who stood behind that veil? And then would come rushing back that scene in the schoolhouse, the smell of the steaming garments, the gases from the lamps, the roar of the stove, the sound of his own voice, strident, dominating, so alien to his present mood, he could only shudder at it.

He was worn out with thinking when he drove into the stable at the Merchants' House and roused up the sleeping hostler, who looked at him suspiciously and demanded pay in advance. This seemed right in his present mood. He was not to be trusted.

When he flung himself face downward on his bed, the turmoil in his brain was still going on. He couldn't hold one thought or feeling long; all seemed slipping like water from his hands.

He had in him great capacity for change, for growth. Circumstances had been against his development thus far, but the time had come when growth seemed to be defeat and failure.

VI

RADBOURN was thinking about him, two days after, as he sat in his friend Judge Brown's law office, poring over a volume of law. He saw that Bacon's treatment had been heroic; he couldn't get the pitiful confusion of the preacher's face out of his mind. But, after all, Bacon's seizing of just that instant was a stroke of genius.

Some one touched him on the arm and he turned.

"Why — Elder — Mr. Pill, how de do? Sit down. Draw up a chair."

There was trouble in the preacher's face. "Can I see you, Radbourn, alone?"

"Certainly; come right into this room. No one will disturb us there."

"Now, what can I do for you?" he said, as they sat down.

"I want to talk to you about — about religion," said Pill, with a little timid pause in his voice.

Radbourn looked grave. "I'm afraid you've come to a dangerous man."

"I want you to tell me what you think. I know you're a student. I want to talk about my case," pursued the preacher, with a curious hesitancy. "I want to ask a few questions on things."

"Very well; sail in. I'll do the best I can," said Radbourn.

"I've been thinking a good deal since that night. I've come to the conclusion that I don't believe what I've been preaching. I thought I did, but I didn't. I don't know *what* I believe. Seems as if the land had slid from under my feet. What am I to do?"

"Say so," replied Radbourn, his eyes kindling. "Say so, and get out of it. There's nothing worse than staying where you are. What have you saved from the general land-slide?"

Pill smiled a little. "I don't know."

"Want me to cross-examine you and see, eh? Very well, here goes." He settled back with a smile. "You believe in square dealing between man and man?"

"Certainly."

"You believe in good deeds, candor, and steadfastness?"

"I do."

"You believe in justice, equality of opportunity, and in liberty?"

"Certainly I do."

"You believe, in short, that a man should do unto others as he'd have others do unto him; think right and live out his thoughts?"

"All that I steadfastly believe."

"Well, I guess your land-slide was mostly imaginary. The face of the eternal rock is laid bare. You didn't recognize it at first, that's all. One question more. You believe in getting at truth?"

"Certainly."

"Well, truth is only found from the generalizations of facts. Before calling a thing true, study carefully all accessible facts. Make your religion practical. The matter-of-fact tone of Bacon would have had no force if you had been preaching an earnest morality in place of an antiquated terrorism."

"I know it, I know it," sighed Pill, looking down.

"Well, now go back and tell 'em so. And then, if you can't keep your place preaching what you do believe, get into something else. For the sake of all morality and manhood, don't go on cursing yourself with hypocrisy."

Mr. Pill took a chew of tobacco rather distractedly, and said: —

"I'd like to ask you a few questions."

"No, not now. You think out your present position yourself. Find out just what you have saved from your land-slide."

The elder man rose; he hardly seemed the same man who had dominated his people a few days before. He turned with still greater embarrassment.

"I want to ask a favor. I'm going back to my family. I'm going to say something of what you've said, to my congregation — but — I'm in debt — and the moment they know I'm a backslider, they're going to bear down on me pretty heavy. I'd like to be independent."

"I see. How much do you need?" mused Radbourn.

"I guess two hundred would stave off the worst of them."

"I guess Brown and I can fix that. Come in again to-night. Or no, I'll bring it round to you."

The two men parted with a silent pressure of the hand that meant more than any words.

When Mr. Pill told his wife that he could preach no more, she cried, and gasped, and scolded till she was in danger of losing her breath entirely. "A guinea-hen sort of a woman" Councill called her. "She can talk more an' say less 'n any woman I ever see," was Bacon's verdict, after she had been at dinner at his house. She was a perpetual irritant.

Mr. Pill silenced her at last with a note of impatience approaching a threat, and drove away to the Corners to make his confession without her. It was Saturday night, and Elder Wheat was preaching as he entered the crowded room. A buzz and mumble of surprise stopped the orator for a few moments, and he shook hands with Mr. Pill dubiously, not knowing what to think of it all, but as he was in the midst of a very effective oratorical scene, he went on.

The silent man at his side felt as if he were witness-

ing a burlesque of himself as he listened to the pitiless
and lurid description of torment which Elder Wheat
poured forth, — the same figures and threats he had used
a hundred times.   He stirred uneasily in his seat, while
the audience paid so little attention that the perspiring
little orator finally called for a hymn, saying : —

"Elder Pill has returned from his unexpected absence,
and will exhort in his proper place."

When the singing ended, Mr. Pill rose, looking more
like himself than since the previous Sunday.   A quiet
resolution was in his eyes and voice as he said : —

"Elder Wheat has more right here than I have.   I
want 'o say that I'm going to give up my church in
Douglass and — " A murmur broke out, which he
silenced with his raised hand.   "I find I don't believe
any longer what I've been believing and preaching.
Hold on ! let me go on.   I don't quite know where I'll
bring up, but I think my religion will simmer down
finally to about this : A full half-bushel to the half-
bushel and sixteen ounces to the pound."   Here two or
three cheered.   "Do unto others as you'd have others
do unto you."   Applause from several, quickly sup-
pressed as the speaker went on, Elder Wheat listening
as if petrified, with his mouth open.

"I'm going out of preaching, at least for the present.
After things get into shape with me again, I may set up
to teach people how to live, but just now I can't do it.
I've got all I can do to instruct myself.   Just one thing
more.   I owe two or three of you here.   I've got the
money for William Bacon, James Bartlett, and John

Jennings. I turn the mare and cutter over to Jacob Bensen, for the note he holds. I hain't got much religion left, but I've got some morality. That's all I want to say now."

When he sat down there was a profound hush; then Bacon arose.

" That's *man's* talk, that is ! An' I jest want 'o say, Andrew Pill, that you kin jest forget you owe me anything.. An' if ye want any help come to me. Y're jest gittun' ready to preach, 'n' I'm ready to give ye my support."

" That's the talk," said Councill. " I'm with ye on that."

Pill shook his head. The painful silence which followed was broken by the effusive voice of Wheat : —

" Let us pray — and remember our lost brother."

The urgings of the people were of no avail. Mr. Pill settled up his affairs and moved to Cresco, where he went back into trade with a friend, and for three years attended silently to his customers, lived down their curiosity, and studied anew the problem of life. Then he moved away, and no one knew whither.

One day last year Bacon met Jennings on the road.

" Heerd anything o' Pill lately ? "

" No, have you ? "

" Waal, yes. Brown told me he ran acrost him down in Eelinoy, doun' well, too."

" In dry goods ? "

" No, preachun'."

" Preachun' ? "

" So Brown said. Kind of a free-f'r-all church, I reckon, from what Jedge told me. Built a new church; fills it twice a Sunday. I'd like to hear him, but he's got t' be too big a gun f'r us. Ben studyun', they say; went t' school."

Jennings drove sadly and thoughtfully on.

" Rather stumps Brother Jennings," laughed Bacon, in a good-humored growl.

A DAY OF GRACE

The grace of God is on you, girl,
He is most glad of every limb ;
His joy is in each glancing curl,
And every dimple pleases Him.

A DAY OF GRACE

Sunday is the day for courtship on the prairie. It has also the piety of cleanliness. It allows the young man to get back to a self-respecting sweetness of person, and enables the girls to look as nature intended, dainty and sweet as posies.

The change from everyday clothing on the part of young workmen like Ben Griswold was more than change; it approached transformation. It took more than courage to go through the change, — it required love.

Ben arose a little later on Sunday morning than on weekdays, but there were the chores to do as usual. The horses must be watered, fed, and curried, and the cows were to milk, but after breakfast Ben threw off the cares of the hired hand. When he came down from the little garret into which the hot August sun streamed redly, he was a changed creature. Clean from tip to toe, newly shaven, wearing a crackling white shirt, a linen collar and a new suit of store clothes, he felt himself a man again, fit to meet maidens.

His partner, being a married man, was slouching around in his tattered and greasy brown denim overalls. He looked at Ben and grinned.

" Got a tag on y'rself ? "

" No, why ? "

"Nobod'y know ye, if anything happened on the road. There's thirty dollars gone to the dogs." He sighed. "Oh, well, you'll get over that, just as I did."

"I hope I won't get over liking to be clean," Ben said a little sourly. "I won't be back to milk."

"Didn't expect ye. That's the very time o' day the girls are purtiest, — just about sundown. Better take Rock. I may want the old team myself."

Ben hitched up and drove off in the warm bright morning, with wonderful elation, clean and self-respecting once more. His freshly shaven face felt cool, and his new suit fitted him well. His heart took on a great resolution, which was to call upon Grace.

The thought of her made his brown hands shake, and he remembered how many times he had sworn to visit her, but had failed of courage, though it seemed she had invited him by word and look to do so.

He overtook Milton Jennings on his way along the poplar-lined lane.

"Hello, Milt, where you bound?"

Milton glanced up with a curious look in his laughing eyes. From the pockets of his long linen duster he drew a handful of beautiful scarlet and yellow Siberian crab-apples.

"See them crabs?"

"Yes, I see 'em."

Milton drew a similar handful out of his left pocket. "See those?"

"What y' going to do with 'em?"

"Take 'em home again."

Something in Milton's voice led him to ask soberly:—
"What did you intend doing with 'em?"
"Present 'em to Miss Cole."
"Well, why didn't y' do it?"
Milton showed his white teeth in a smile that was frankly derisive of himself.

"Well, when I got over there I found young Conley's sorrel hitched to one post and Walt Brown's gray hitched to the other. I went in, but I didn't stay long; in fact, I didn't sit down. I was afraid those infernal apples would roll out o' my pockets. I was afraid they'd find out I brought 'em over there for Miss Cole, like the darn fool I was."

They both laughed heartily. Milton was always as severe upon himself as upon any one else.

"That's tough," said Ben, "but climb in, and let's go to Sunday-school."

Milton got in, and they ate the apples as they rode along.

The Grove schoolhouse was the largest in the township, and was the only one with a touch of redeeming grace. It was in a lovely spot; great oaks stood all about, and back of it the woods grew thick, and a clear creek gurgled over its limestone bed not far away.

To Ben and Milton there was a wondrous charm about the Grove schoolhouse. It was the one place where the boys and girls met in garments disassociated from toil. Sundays in summer, and on winter nights at lyceums or protracted meetings, the boys came to

see the girls in their bright dresses, with their clear
and (so it seemed) scornful bright eyes.

All through the service Ben sat where he could see
Grace by turning his head, but he had not the courage
to do so. Once or twice he caught a glimpse of the
curve of her cheek and the delicate lines of her ear,
and a suffocating throb came into his throat.

He wanted to ask her to go with him down to
Cedarville to the Methodist camp-meeting, but he
knew it was impossible. He could not even say "good
day" when she took pains to pass near him after church.
He nodded like a great idiot, all ease and dignity lost,
his throat too dry and hot to utter a sound.

He cursed his shyness as he went out after his horse.
He saw her picking her dainty way up the road with
Conrad Sieger walking by her side. What made it
worse for Ben was a dim feeling that she liked him,
and would go with him if he had the courage to ask her.

"Well, Ben," said Milton, "it's settled, we go to
Rock River to-night to the camp-meeting. Did you
ask Grace?"

"No, she's going with Con. It's just my blasted
luck."

"That's too bad. Well, come with us. Take
Maud."

As he rode away Ben passed Grace on the road.

"Going to the camp-meeting, Con?" asked Milton,
in merry voice.

"I guess so," said Conrad, a handsome, but slow-
witted German.

As they went on Ben could have wept. His keener perception told him there was a look of appeal in Grace's upturned eyes.

He made a poor companion at dinner, and poor plain Maud knew his mind was elsewhere. She was used to that and accepted it with a pathetic attempt to color it differently.

They got away about five o'clock.

Ben drove the team, driving took his mind off his weakness and failure; while Milton in the seclusion of the back seat of the carryall was happy with Amelia Turner.

It was growing dark as they entered upon the curving road along the river which was a relief from the rectangular and sun-smitten roads of the prairie. They lingered under the great oaks and elms which shaded them. It would have been perfect Ben thought, if Grace had been beside him in Maud's place.

He wondered how he should manage to speak to Grace. There was a time when it seemed easier. Now the consciousness of his love made the simplest question seem like the great question of all.

Other teams were on the road, some returning, some going. A camp-meeting had come to be an annual amusement, like a circus, and young people from all over the country drove down on Sundays, as if to some celebration with fireworks.

"There's the lane," said Milton. "See that team goin' in?"

Ben pulled up and they looked at it doubtfully. It

looked dangerously miry. It was quite dark now and
Ben said : —

"That's a scaly piece of road."

"Oh, that's all right. Hark!"

As they listened they could hear the voice of the
exhorter nearly a mile away. It pushed across the
cool spaces with a wild and savage sound. The young
people thrilled with excitement.

Insects were singing in the grass. Frogs with
deepening chorus seemed to announce the coming of
night, and above these peaceful sounds came the wild
shouts of the far-off preacher, echoing through the
cool green arches of the splendid grove.

The girls became silent, as the voice grew louder.

Lights appeared ahead, and the road led up a slight
hill to a gate. Ben drove on under a grove of oaks,
past dimly lighted tents, whose open flaps showed
tumbled beds and tables laden with crockery. Heavy
women were moving about inside, their shadows
showing against the tent walls like figures in a panto-
mime.

The young people alighted in curious silence. As
they stood a moment, tying the team, the preacher lifted
his voice in a brazen, clanging, monotonous reiteration
of worn phrases.

"Come to the *Lord!* Come *now!* Come to the
light! Jesus will give it! *Now* is the appointed time,
— come to the *light!*"

From a tent near by arose the groaning, gasping,
gurgling scream of a woman in mortal agony.

" O my God ! "

It was charged with the most piercing distress. It cut to the heart's palpitating centre like a poniard thrust. It had murder and outrage in it.

The girls clutched Ben and Milton. " Oh, let's go home ! "

" No, let's go and see what it all is."

The girls hung close to the arms of the young men and they went down to the tent and looked in.

It was filled with a motley throng of people, most of them seated on circling benches. A fringe of careless or scoffing onlookers stood back against the tent wall. Many of them were strangers to Ben.

Occasionally a Norwegian farm-hand, or a bevy of young people from some near district, lifted the flap and entered with curious or laughing or insolent faces.

The tent was lighted dimly by kerosene lamps, hung in brackets against the poles, and by stable lanterns set here and there upon the benches.

Ben and Milton ushered the girls in and seated them a little way back. The girls smiled, but only faintly. The undertone of women's cries moved them in spite of their scorn of it all.

" What cursed foolishness ! " said Ben to Milton.

Milton smiled, but did not reply. He only nodded toward the exhorter, a man with a puffy jumble of features and the form of a gladiator, who was uttering wild and explosive phrases.

" Oh, my friends ! I bless the Lord for the SHALL in the word. You SHALL get light. You SHALL be saved. Oh, the SHALL in the word! You SHALL be redeemed!"

As he grew more excited, his hoarse voice rose in furious screams, as if he were defying hell's legions. Foam lay on his lips and flew from his mouth. At every repetition of the word " shall " he struck the desk a resounding blow with his great palm.

" He's a hard hitter," said Milton.

At length he leaped, apparently in uncontrollable excitement, upon the mourners' bench, and ran up and down close to the listening, moaning audience. He walked with a furious rhythmic, stamping action, like a Sioux in the war dance. Wild cries burst from his audience, antiphonal with his own.

" He 'SHALL' send light ! "

" *Send Thy arrows, O Lord.*"

" O God, come ! "

" He 'SHALL' keep His word! "

One old negro woman, fat, powerful, and gloomy, suddenly arose and uttered a scream that had the dignity and savagery of a mountain lion's cry. It rang far out into the night.

The exhorter continued his mad, furious, thumping, barbaric walk.

Behind him a row of other exhorters sat, a relay ready to leap to his aid. They urged on the tumult with wild cries.

" A-men, brother."

" YES, brother, YES!" clapping their hands in rhythm.

The exhorter redoubled his fury. He was like a jaded actor rising at applause, carried out of his self-command.

Out of the obscure tumult of faces and tossing hands there came at last certain recognizable features. The people were mainly farming folks of the more ignorant sort, rude in dress and bearing, hard and bent with toil. They were recognizably of a class subject to these low forms of religious excitement which were once well-nigh universal.

The outer fringe continued to smile scornfully and to jest, yet they were awed, in a way, by this suddenly revealed deep of barbaric emotion.

The girls were appalled by the increasing clangor. Milton was amused, but Ben grew bitter. Something strong came out in him, too. His lip curled in disgust.

Suddenly, out of the level space of bowed shoulders, tossing hands, and frenzied, upturned faces, a young girl leaped erect. She was strong and handsome, powerful in the waist and shoulders. Her hair was braided like a child's, and fell down her back in a single strand. Her head was girlish, but her face looked old and drawn and tortured.

She moaned pitifully; she clapped her hands with wild gestures, ending in a quivering motion. The action grew to lightning-like quickness. Her head seemed to set in its socket. Her whole body stiffened. Gasping moans came from her clenched teeth as she fell to the ground and rolled under the seats, wallowing in the muddy straw and beating her feet upon the ground like a dying partridge.

The people crowded about her, but the preacher, roared above the tumult : —

" Si' down !   Never mind that party.   She's all right; she's in the hands of the Lord ! "

The people settled into their seats, and the wild tumult went on again.   Ben rose to go over where the girl was and the others followed.

A young man seated by the struggling sinner held her hand and fanned her with his hat, while some girl friends, scared and sobbing, kept the tossing limbs covered.   She rolled from side to side restlessly, thrusting forth her tongue as if her throat were dry.   She looked like a dying animal.

Maud clung to Milton.

" Oh, can't something be done ? "

" Her soul is burdened for *you !* " cried a wild old woman to the impassive youth who clung to the frenzied girl's hand.

A moment later, as the demoniacal chorus of yells, songs, incantations, shrieks, groans, and prayers swelled high, a farmer's wife on the left uttered a hoarse cry and stiffened and fell backward upon the ground.   She rolled her head from side to side.   Her eyes turned in ; her lips wore a maniac's laugh, and her troubled brow made her look like the death mask of a tortured murderer, the hell horror frozen on it.

She sank at last into a hideous calm, with her strained and stiffened hands pointing weirdly up.   She was like marble.   She did not move a hair's breadth during the next two hours.

Over to the left a young man leaped to his feet with a scream : —

" Jesus, *Jesus*, JESUS ! "

The great negress caught him in her arms as he fell, and laid him down, then leaped up and down, shrieking : —

" O Jesus, come. Come, God's Lamb ! "

Around her a dozen women took up her cry. Most of them had no voices. Their horrifying screams had become hoarse hisses, yet still they strove. Scores of voices were mixed in the pandemonium of prayer.

All order was lost. Three of the preachers now stood shouting before the mourners' bench, two were in the aisles.

One came down the aisle toward the girl with the braided hair. As he came he prayed. Foam was on his lips, but his eyes were cool and calculating; they betrayed him.

As he came he fixed his gaze upon a woman seated near the prostrate girl, and with a horrible outcry the victim leaped into the air and stiffened as if smitten with epilepsy. She fell against some scared boys, who let her fall, striking her head against the seats. She too rolled down upon the straw and lay beside her sister. Both had round, pretty, but childish faces.

Milton's party retreated. They smiled no more; they were horror-stricken.

Squads of " workers " now moved down the aisles; in one they surrounded two people, a tall, fair girl and a young man.

"Why, it's Grace!" exclaimed Maud.

Ben turned quickly, "Where?"

They pointed her out.

"She can't get away. See! Oh, boys, don't let them —"

Ben pushed his way toward her, his face set in a fierce frown, bitter, desperate.

Grace stood silently beside one of the elders; a woman exhorter stood before her. Conrad, overawed, had fallen into a trembling stupor; Grace was defenseless.

The elder's hand hovered over her head, on her face a deadly pallor had settled, her eyes were cast down, she breathed painfully and trembled from head to foot. She was about to fall, when Ben set his eyes upon her.

"Get out o' my way," he shouted, shouldering up the aisle. His words had oaths, his fists were like mauls.

"Grace!" he cried, and she heard. She looked up and saw him coming; the red flamed over her face.

The power of the preacher was gone.

"Let me go," she cried, trying to wring herself loose.

"You are going to hell. You are lost if you do not —"

"God damn ye. Get out o' way. I'll kill ye if you lay a hand on her."

With one thrust Ben cleared her tormentor from her arm. For one moment the wordless young man looked into her eyes; then she staggered toward him. He faced the preacher.

"I'd smash hell out o' you for a leather cent," he said. In the tumult his words were lost, but the look on his face was enough. The exhorter fell away.

Their retreat was unnoted in the tumult. At the door they looked back for an instant at the scene.

At the mourners' bench were six victims in all stages of induced catalepsy, one man with head flung back, one with his hands pointing, fixed in furious appeal. Another with bowed head was being worked upon by a brother of hypnotic appeal. He struck with downward, positive gestures on either side of the victim's head.

Over another the negress towered, screaming with panther-like ferocity : —

"Git under de blood! Git under de blood!"

As she screamed she struck down at the mourner with her clenched fist. On her face was the grin of a wildcat.

Out under the cool, lofty oaks, the outcry was more inexpressibly hellish, because overhead the wind rustled the sweet green leaves, crickets were chirping, and the scent of flowering fields of buckwheat was in the air.

Grace grew calmer, but she clung with strange weakness to her lover. She felt he had saved her from something, she did not know what, but it was something terrifying to look back upon.

Conrad was forgotten — set aside. Ben bundled him into the carryall and took his place with Grace. He no longer hesitated, argued, or apologized. He had claimed his own.

On the long ride home, Grace lay within his right arm, and the young man's tongue was unchained. He, talked, and his spirit grew tender and manly and husbandlike, as he told his plans and his hopes. Hell was very far away, and Heaven was very near.

A FARMER'S WIFE

"Born an' scrubbed, suffered and died."
That's all you need to say, elder.
　　Never mind sayin' "made a bride,"
Nor when her hair got gray.
　　Jest say, born 'n worked t' death;
　　That fits it, — save y'r breath.

I knew M'tildy when a girl,
'N a darn purty girl she was!
　　Her hair was shiny 'n full o' curl,
An' her eyes a kind o' spring-day blue.
　　O, I know! Courted her once m'self,
　　Till Brown he laid me on the shelf.

I've seen that woman once a week
Ever since that very day in church,
　　When Ben turned round 'n kissed her cheek
And the preacher knelt to pray.
　　I've watched her growing old so fast —
　　Her breath jest *flickered* toward the last.

Made me think of a clock run down,
Sure 's y're born, that woman did;
　　A-workin' away for old Ben Brown
Patient as a Job an' meek as a kid,
　　Till she sort o' stopped one day —
　　Heart quit tickin', a feller 'd say.

Wasn't old, nuther, forty-six — No,
Jest got humpt, an' thin an' gray,
   Washin' an' churnin' an' sweepin', by Joe,
F'r fourteen hours or more a day.
   Brats o' sickly children every year
   To drag the life plum out o' her.

Worked to death.   Starved to death.
Died f'r lack of air an' sun —
   Dyin' f'r rest, and f'r jest a breath
O' simple praise for what she'd done.
   An' many 's the woman this very day,
   Elder, dyin' slow in that same way.

LUCRETIA BURNS

LUCRETIA BURNS

I

LUCRETIA BURNS had never been handsome, even in her days of early girlhood, and now she was middle-aged, distorted with work and child-bearing, and looking faded and worn as one of the boulders that lay beside the pasture fence near where she sat milking a large white cow.

She had no shawl or hat and no shoes, for it was still muddy in the little yard, where the cattle stood patiently fighting the flies and mosquitoes swarming into their skins, already wet with blood. The evening was oppressive with its heat, and a ring of just-seen thunder-heads gave premonitions of an approaching storm.

She rose from the cow's side at last, and, taking her pails of foaming milk, staggered toward the gate. The two pails hung from her lean arms, her bare feet slipped on the filthy ground, her greasy and faded calico dress showed her tired and swollen ankles, and the mosquitoes swarmed mercilessly on her neck and bedded themselves in her colorless hair.

The children were quarrelling at the well, and the sound of blows could be heard. Calves were querulously calling for their milk, and little turkeys, lost in a tangle of grass, were piping plaintively.

The sun just setting struck through a long, low rift, like a boy peeping beneath the eaves of a huge roof. Its light brought out Lucretia's face as she leaned her sallow forehead on the top bar of the gate and looked toward the west.

It was a pitifully worn, almost tragic face — long, thin, sallow, hollow-eyed. The mouth had long since lost the power to shape itself into a kiss, and had a droop at the corners which seemed to announce a breaking-down at any moment into a despairing wail. The collarless neck and sharp shoulders showed painfully.

She felt vaguely that the night was beautiful. The setting sun, the noise of frogs, the nocturnal insects beginning to pipe — all in some way called her girlhood back to her, though there was little in her girlhood to give her pleasure. Her large gray eyes grew round, deep, and wistful as she saw the illimitable craggy clouds grow crimson, roll slowly up, and fire at the top. A childish scream recalled her.

"Oh, my soul!" she half groaned, half swore, as she lifted her milk and hurried to the well. Arriving there, she cuffed the children right and left with all her remaining strength, saying in justification : —

"My soul! can't you — you young 'uns, give me a minute's peace? Land knows, I'm almost gone up; washin', an' milkin' six cows, and tendin' you, and cookin' f'r *him*, ought 'o be enough f'r one day! Sadie, you let him drink now 'r I'll slap your head off, you hateful thing! Why can't you behave, when you know I'm jest about dead?" She was weeping now, with

nervous weakness.   " Where's y'r pa ? " she asked
after a moment, wiping her eyes with her apron.

One of the group, the one cuffed last, sniffed out, in
rage and grief : —

" He's in the corn-field ; where'd ye s'pose he was ? "

" Good land ! why don't the man work all night ?
Sile, you put that dipper in that milk agin, an' I'll
whack you till your head'll swim !   Sadie, le' go Pet, an'
go 'n get them turkeys out of the grass 'fore it gits
dark !   Bob, you go tell y'r dad if he wants the rest o'
them cows milked he's got 'o do it himself.   I jest
can't, and what's more, I *won't*," she ended, rebel-
liously.

Having strained the milk and fed the children, she
took some skimmed milk from the cans and started to
feed the calves bawling strenuously behind the barn.
The eager and unruly brutes pushed and struggled
to get into the pails all at once, and in consequence
spilt nearly all of the milk on the ground.   This was
the last trial; the woman fell down on the damp grass
and moaned and sobbed like a crazed thing.   The
children came to seek her and stood around like little
partridges, looking at her in scared silence, till at last
the little one began to wail.   Then the mother rose
wearily to her feet, and walked slowly back toward the
house.

She heard Burns threshing his team at the well, with
the sound of oaths.   He was tired, hungry, and ill-tem-
pered, but she was too desperate to care.   His poor,
overworked team did not move quickly enough for him,

and his extra long turn in the corn had made him dangerous. His eyes gleamed wrathfully from his dust-laid face.

" Supper ready ? " he growled.

" Yes, two hours ago."

" Well, I can't help it ! " he said, understanding her reproach. " That devilish corn is gettin' too tall to plough again, and I've got 'o go through it to-morrow or not at all. Cows milked ? "

" Part of 'em."

" How many left ? "

" Three."

" Hell !　Which three ? "

" Spot, and Brin, and Cherry."

" *Of* course, left the three worst ones. I'll be damned if I milk a cow to-night. I don't see why you play out jest the nights I need ye most." Here he kicked a child out of the way. " Git out o' that ! Hain't you got no sense ?　I'll learn ye — "

" Stop that, Sim Burns," cried the woman, snatching up the child. " You're a reg'lar ol' hyeny, — that's what you are," she added defiantly, roused at last from her lethargy.

" You're a — beauty, that's what *you* are," he said, pitilessly. " Keep your brats out f'um under my feet." And he strode off to the barn after his team, leaving her with a fierce hate in her heart. She heard him yelling at his team in their stalls : " Git around there, damn yeh."

The children had had their supper ; so she took them

to bed. She was unusually tender to them, for she wanted to make up in some way for her previous harshness. The ferocity of her husband had shown up her own petulant temper hideously, and she sat and sobbed in the darkness a long time beside the cradle where little Pet slept.

She heard Burns come growling in and tramp about, but she did not rise. The supper was on the table; he could wait on himself. There was an awful feeling at her heart as she sat there and the house grew quiet. She thought of suicide in a vague way; of somehow taking her children in her arms and sinking into a lake somewhere, where she would never more be troubled, where she could sleep forever, without toil or hunger.

Then she thought of the little turkeys wandering in the grass, of the children sleeping at last, of the quiet, wonderful stars. Then she thought of the cows left unmilked, and listened to them stirring uneasily in the yard. She rose, at last, and stole forth. She could not rid herself of the thought that they would suffer. She knew what the dull ache in the full breasts of a mother was, and she could not let them stand at the bars all night moaning for relief.

The mosquitoes had gone, but the frogs and katydids still sang, while over in the west Venus shone. She was a long time milking the cows; her hands were so tired she had often to stop and rest them, while the tears fell unheeded into the pail. She saw and felt little of the external as she sat there. She thought in vague retrospect of how sweet it seemed the first time Sim came to see her; of the many rides to town with him when he was an accepted lover; of the few things he had given her — a coral breastpin and a ring.

She felt no shame at her present miserable appearance; she was past personal pride. She hardly felt as if the tall, strong girl, attractive with health and hope, could be the same soul as the woman who now sat in utter despair listening to the heavy breathing of the happy cows, grateful for the relief from their burden of milk.

She contrasted her lot with that of two or three women that she knew (not a very high standard), who kept hired help, and who had fine houses of four or five rooms. Even the neighbors were better off than she, for they didn't have such quarrels. But she wasn't to blame — Sim didn't — Then her mind changed to a dull resentment against " things." Everything seemed against her.

She rose at last and carried her second load of milk to the well, strained it, washed out the pails, and, after bathing her tired feet in a tub that stood there, she put on a pair of horrible shoes, without stockings, and crept stealthily into the house. Sim did not hear her as she slipped up the stairs to the little low unfinished chamber beside her oldest children. She could not bear to sleep near *him* that n'ght, — she wanted a chance to sob herself to quiet.

As for Sim, he was a little disturbed, but would as soon have cut off his head as acknowledged himself in the wrong. As he went to bed, and found her still away, he yelled up the stairway: —

"Say, old woman, ain't ye comin' to bed?" Upon
receiving no answer he rolled his aching body into the
creaking bed. "Do as y' damn please about it. If y'
want to sulk y' can." And in such wise the family
grew quiet in sleep, while the moist, warm air pulsed
with the ceaseless chime of the crickets.

II

When Sim Burns woke the next morning he felt a
sharper twinge of remorse. It was not a broad or well-
defined feeling — just a sense that he had been unduly
irritable, not that on the whole he was not in the right.
Little Pet lay with the warm June sunshine filling his
baby eyes, curiously content in striking at flies that
buzzed around his little mouth.

The man thrust his dirty, naked feet into his huge
boots, and, without washing his face or combing his hair,
went out to the barn to do his chores.

He was a type of the average prairie farmer, and his
whole surrounding was typical of the time. He had a
quarter-section of fine level land, bought with incredible
toil, but his house was a little box-like structure, costing,
perhaps, five hundred dollars. It had three rooms and
the ever-present summer kitchen at the back. It was
unpainted and had no touch of beauty, — a mere box.

His stable was built of slabs and banked and covered
with straw. It looked like a den, was low and long,
and had but one door in the end. The cow-yard held
ten or fifteen cattle of various kinds, while a few calves

were bawling from a pen near by.   Behind the barn, on
the west and north, was a fringe of willows forming a
"wind-break."   A few broken and discouraged fruit trees,
standing here and there among the weeds, formed the
garden.   In short, he was spoken of by his neighbors as
" a hard-working cuss, and tol'ably well fixed."

No grace had come or ever could come into his life.
Back of him were generations of men like himself,
whose main business had been to work hard, live mis-
erably, and beget children to take their places when
they died.

His courtship had been delayed so long on account of
poverty that it brought little of humanizing emotion into
his life.   He never mentioned his love-life now, or if he
did, it was only to sneer obscenely at it.   He had long
since ceased to kiss his wife or even speak kindly to her.
There was no longer any sanctity to life or love.   He
chewed tobacco and toiled on from year to year without
any very clearly defined idea of the future.   His life was
mainly regulated from without.

He was tall, dark, and strong, in a flat-chested, slouching sort of way, and had grown neglectful of even
decency in his dress.   He wore the American farmer's
customary outfit of rough brown pants, hickory shirt, and
greasy wool hat.   It differed from his neighbors' mainly
in being a little dirtier and more ragged.   His grimy
hands were broad and strong as the clutch of a bear, and
he was a " terrible feller to turn off work," as Councill
said.   " I'd ruther have Sim Burns work for me one day
than some men three.   He's a linger."   He worked

with unusual speed this morning, and ended by milking all the cows himself as a sort of savage penance for his misdeeds the previous evening, muttering in self-defence : —

"Seems 's if ever' cussid thing piles on to me at once. That corn, the road-tax, and hayin' comin' on, and now *she* gits her back up — "

When he went back to the well he sloshed himself thoroughly in the horse-trough and went to the house. He found breakfast ready, but his wife was not in sight. The older children were clamoring around the uninviting breakfast table, spread with cheap ware and with boiled potatoes and fried salt pork as the principal dishes.

"Where's y'r ma?" he asked, with a threatening note in his voice, as he sat down by the table.

"She's in the bedroom."

He rose and pushed open the door. The mother sat with the babe in her lap, looking out of the window down across the superb field of timothy, moving like a lake of purple water. She did not look around. She only grew rigid. Her thin neck throbbed with the pulsing of blood to her head.

"What's got into you *now?*" he said, brutally. "Don't be a fool. Come out and eat breakfast with me, an' take care o' y'r young ones."

She neither moved nor made a sound. With an oath he turned on his heel and went out to the table. Eating his breakfast in his usual wolfish fashion, he went out into the hot sun with his team and riding-plough, not a little disturbed by this new phase of his wife's "cantankerousness." He ploughed steadily and sullenly all the forenoon, in the terrific heat and dust. The air was full of tempestuous threats, still and sultry, one of those days when work is a punishment. When he came in at noon he found things the same — dinner on the table, but his wife out in the garden with the youngest child.

"I c'n stand it as long as *she* can," he said to himself, in the hearing of the children, as he pushed back from the table and went back to work.

When he had finished the field of corn it was after sundown, and he came up to the house, hot, dusty, his shirt wringing wet with sweat, and his neck aching with the work of looking down all day at the corn-rows. His mood was still stern. The multitudinous lift, and stir, and sheen of the wide, green field had been lost upon him.

"I wonder if she's milked them cows," he muttered to himself. He gave a sigh of relief to find she had. But she had done so not for his sake, but for the sake of the poor, patient dumb brutes.

When he went to the bedroom after supper, he found that the cradle and his wife's few little boxes and parcels — poor, pathetic properties! — had been removed to the garret, which they called a chamber, and he knew he was to sleep alone again.

"She'll git over it, I guess." He was very tired, but he didn't feel quite comfortable enough to sleep. The air was oppressive. His shirt, wet in places, and stiff with dust in other places, oppressed him more than usual; so he rose and removed it, getting a clean one out of a drawer. This was an unusual thing for him, for he usually slept in the same shirt which he wore in his day's work; but it was Saturday night, and he felt justified in the extravagance.

In the meanwhile poor Lucretia was brooding over her life in a most dangerous fashion. All she had done and suffered for Simeon Burns came back to her till she wondered how she had endured it all. All day long in the midst of the glorious summer landscape she brooded.

"I hate him," she thought, with a fierce blazing up through the murk of her musing. "I hate t' live. But they ain't no hope. I'm tied down. I can't leave the children, and I ain't got no money. I couldn't make a living out in the world. I ain't never seen anything an' don't know anything."

She was too simple and too unknowing to speculate on the loss of her beauty, which would have brought her competency once — if sold in the right market. As she lay in her little attic bed, she was still sullenly thinking, wearily thinking of her life. She thought of a poor old horse which Sim had bought once, years before, and put to the plough when it was too old and weak to work. She could see her again as in a vision, that poor old mare, with sad head drooping, toiling, toiling, till at last she could no longer move, and lying down under the harness in the furrow, groaned under the whip, — and died.

Then she wondered if her own numbness and despair meant death, and she held her breath to think harder upon it. She concluded at last, grimly, that she didn't care — only for the children.

The air was frightfully close in the little attic, and she heard the low mutter of the rising storm in the west. She forgot her troubles a little, listening to the far-off gigantic footsteps of the tempest.

Boom, boom, boom, it broke nearer and nearer, as if a vast cordon of cannon was being drawn around the horizon. Yet she was conscious only of pleasure. She had no fear. At last came the sweep of cool, fragrant storm-wind, a short and sudden dash of rain, and then in the cool, sweet hush which followed, the worn and weary woman fell into a deep sleep.

III

WHEN she woke the younger children were playing about on the floor in their night-clothes, and little Pet was sitting in a square of sunshine, intent on one of his shoes. He was too young to know how poor and squalid his surroundings were, — the patch of sunshine flung on the floor glorified it all. He — little animal — was happy.

The poor of the Western prairies lie almost as unhealthily close together as do the poor of the city tenements. In the small hut of the peasant there is as little chance to escape close and tainting contact as in the coops and dens of the North End of proud Boston. In the midst of oceans of land, floods of sunshine and gulfs of verdure, the farmer lives in two or three small rooms. Poverty's eternal cordon is ever round the poor.

"Ma, why didn't you sleep with Pap last night?" asked Bob, the seven-year-old, when he saw she was awake at last. She flushed a dull red.

"You hush, will yeh? Because — I — it was too warm — and there was a storm comin'. You never mind askin' such questions. Is he gone out?"

"Yup. I heerd him callin' the pigs. It's Sunday, ain't it, ma?"

The fact seemed to startle her.

"Why, yes, so it is! Wal! Now, Sadie, you jump up an' dress quick 's y' can, an' Bob an' Sile, you run down an' bring s'm' water," she commanded, in nervous haste, beginning to dress. In the middle of the room there was scarce space to stand beneath the rafters.

When Sim came in for his breakfast he found it on the table, but his wife was absent.

"Where's y'r ma?" he asked, with a little less of the growl in his voice.

"She's upstairs with Pet."

The man ate his breakfast in dead silence, till at last Bob ventured to say : —

"What makes ma ac' so?"

"Shut up!" was the brutal reply. The children began to take sides with the mother — all but the oldest girl, who was ten years old. To her the father turned now for certain things to be done, treating her in his rough fashion as a housekeeper, and the girl felt flattered and docile accordingly.

They were pitiably clad; like many farm-children, indeed, they could hardly be said to be clad at all. Sadie had on but two garments, a sort of undershirt of cotton and a faded calico dress, out of which her bare, yellow little legs protruded, lamentably dirty and covered with scratches.

The boys also had two garments, a hickory shirt and a pair of pants like their father's, made out of brown denim by the mother's never-resting hands — hands that in sleep still sewed, and skimmed, and baked, and churned. The boys had gone to bed without washing their feet, which now looked like toads, calloused, brown, and chapped.

Part of this the mother saw with her dull eyes as she came down, after seeing the departure of Sim up the road with the cows. It was a beautiful Sunday morning, and the woman might have sung like a bird if men had been as kind to her as Nature. But she looked dully out upon the seas of ripe grasses, tangled and flashing with dew, out of which the bobolinks and larks sprang. The glorious winds brought her no melody, no perfume, no respite from toil and care.

She thought of the children she saw in the town, — children of the merchant and banker, clean as little dolls, the boys in knickerbocker suits, the girls in dainty white dresses, — and a vengeful bitterness sprang up in her heart. She soon put the dishes away, but felt too tired and listless to do more.

"Taw-bay-wies! Pet want ta-aw-bay-wies!" cried the little one, tugging at her dress.

Listlessly, mechanically she took him in her arms, and went out into the garden, which was fragrant and sweet with dew and sun. After picking some berries for him, she sat down on the grass under the row of cottonwoods, and sank into a kind of lethargy. A kingbird chattered and shrieked overhead, the grass-hoppers buzzed in the grasses, strange insects with ventriloquistic voices sang all about her — she could not tell where.

"Ma, can't I put on my clean dress?" insisted Sadie.

"I don't care," said the brooding woman, darkly. "Leave me alone."

Oh, if she could only lie here forever, escaping all pain and weariness! The wind sang in her ears; the great clouds, beautiful as heavenly ships, floated far above in the vast, dazzling deeps of blue sky; the birds rustled and chirped around her; leaping insects buzzed and clattered in the grass and in the vines and bushes. The goodness and glory of God was in the very air, the bitterness and oppression of man in every line of her face.

But her quiet was broken by Sadie, who came leaping like a fawn down through the grass.

"Oh, ma, Aunt Maria and Uncle William are coming. They've jest turned in."

"I don't care if they be!" she answered in the same dully irritated way. "What're they comin' here to-day for, I wan' to know." She stayed there immovably, till Mrs. Councill came down to see her, piloted by two or three of the children. Mrs. Councill, a jolly, large-framed woman, smiled brightly, and greeted her in a loud, jovial

H

voice. She made the mistake of taking the whole matter lightly; her tone amounted to ridicule.

"Sim says you've been having a tantrum, Creeshy. Don't know what for, he says."

"He don't," said the wife, with a sullen flash in her eyes. "*He* don't know why! Well, then, you just tell him what I say. I've lived in hell long enough. I'm done. I've slaved here day in and day out f'r twelve years without pay, — not even a decent word. I've worked like no nigger ever worked 'r could work and live. I've given him all I had, 'r ever expect to have. I'm wore out. My strength is gone, my patience is gone. I'm done with it, — that's a *part* of what's the matter."

"My sakes, Lucreeshy! You mustn't talk that way."

"But I *will*," said the woman, as she supported herself on one palm and raised the other. "I've *got* to talk that way." She was ripe for an explosion like this. She seized upon it with eagerness. "They ain't no use o' livin' this way, anyway. I'd take poison if it wa'n't f'r the young ones."

"Lucreeshy Burns!"

"Oh, I mean it."

"Land sakes alive, I b'lieve you're goin' crazy!"

"I shouldn't wonder if I was. I've had enough t' drive an Indian crazy. Now you jest go off an' leave me 'lone. I ain't no mind to visit, — they ain't no way out of it' and I'm tired o' trying to *find* a way. Go off an' let me be."

Her tone was so bitterly hopeless that the great, jolly

face of Mrs. Councill stiffened into a look of horror such as she had not known for years. The children, in two separate groups, could be heard rioting. Bees were humming around the clover in the grass, and the king-bird chattered ceaselessly from the Lombardy poplar tip. Both women felt all this peace and beauty of the morning dimly, and it disturbed Mrs. Councill because the other was so impassive under it all. At last, after a long and thoughtful pause, Mrs. Councill asked a question whose answer she knew would decide it all — asked it very kindly and softly : —

"Creeshy, are you comin' in ? "

"No," was the short and sullenly decisive answer. Mrs. Councill knew that was the end, and so rose with a sigh, and went away.

"Wal, good-by," she said, simply.

Looking back, she saw Lucretia lying at length, with closed eyes and hollow cheeks. She seemed to be sleeping, half buried in the grass. She did not look up nor reply to her sister-in-law, whose life was one of toil and trouble also, but not so hard and helpless as Lucretia's. By contrast with most of her neighbors, she seemed comfortable.

"Sim Burns, what you ben doin' to that woman ? " she burst out, as she waddled up to where the two men were sitting under a cottonwood tree, talking and whit-tling after the manner of farmers.

"Nawthin' 's fur 's I know," answered Burns, not quite honestly, and looking uneasy.

"You needn't try t' git out of it like that, Sim Burns,"

replied his sister. "That woman never got into that fit f'r *nawthin'*."

"Wal, if you know more about it than I do, whadgy ask *me* fur?" he replied, angrily.

"Tut, tut!" put in Councill, "hold y'r horses! Don't git on y'r ear, children! Keep cool, and don't spile y'r shirts. Most likely you're all t' blame. Keep cool an' swear less."

"Wal, I'll bet Sim's more to blame than she is. Why, they ain't a harder-workin' woman in the hull State of Ioway than she is —"

"Except Marm Councill."

"Except nobody. Look at her, jest skin and bones."

Councill chuckled in his vast way. "That's so, mother; measured in that way, she leads over you. You git fat on it."

She smiled a little, her indignation oozing away. She never "*could* stay mad," her children were accustomed to tell her. Burns refused to talk any more about the matter, and the visitors gave it up, and got out their team and started for home, Mrs. Councill firing this parting shot : —

"The best thing you can do to-day is t' let her alone. Mebbe the children 'll bring her round ag'in. If she does come round, you see 't you treat her a little more 's y' did when you was a-courtin' her."

"This way," roared Councill, putting his arm around his wife's waist. She boxed his ears, while he guffawed and clucked at his team.

Burns took a measure of salt and went out into the

pasture to salt the cows. On the sunlit slope of the field, where the cattle came running and bawling to meet him, he threw down the salt in handfuls, and then lay down to watch them as they eagerly licked it up, even gnawing a bare spot in the sod in their eagerness to get it all.

Burns was not a drinking man; he was hard-working, frugal; in fact, he had no extravagances except his tobacco. His clothes he wore until they all but dropped from him; and he worked in rain and mud, as well as dust and sun. It was this suffering and toiling all to no purpose that made him sour and irritable. He didn't see why he should have so little after so much hard work.

He was puzzled to account for it all. His mind — the average mind — was weary with trying to solve an insoluble problem. His neighbors, who had got along a little better than himself, were free with advice and suggestion as to the cause of his persistent poverty.

Old man Bacon, the hardest-working man in the county, laid it to Burns's lack of management. Jim Butler, who owned a dozen farms (which he had taken on mortgages), and who had got rich by buying land at government price and holding for a rise, laid all such cases as Burns's to " lack of enterprise, foresight."

But the larger number, feeling themselves in the same boat with Burns, said : —

" I d' know. Seems as if things get worse an' worse. Corn an' wheat gittin' cheaper 'n' cheaper. Machinery eatin' up profits — got to *have* machinery to harvest the cheap grain, an' then the machinery eats up profits. Taxes goin' up. Devil to pay all round; I d' know what in thunder *is* the matter."

The Democrats said protection was killing the farmers; the Republicans said no. The Grangers growled about the middle-men; the Greenbackers said there wasn't circulating medium enough, and, in the midst of it all, hard-working, discouraged farmers, like Simeon Burns, worked on, unable to find out what really was the matter.

And there, on this beautiful Sabbath morning, Sim sat and thought and thought, till he rose with an oath and gave it up.

IV

It was hot and brilliant again the next morning as Douglas Radbourn drove up the road with Lily Graham, the teacher of the school in the little white schoolhouse. It was blazing hot, even though not yet nine o'clock, and the young farmers ploughing beside the fence looked longingly and somewhat bitterly at Radbourn seated in a fine top-buggy beside a beautiful creature in lace and cambric.

Very beautiful the town-bred " schoolma'am " looked to those grimy, sweaty fellows, superb fellows too, physically, with bare red arms and leather-colored faces. She was as if builded of the pink and white clouds soaring far up there in the morning sky. So cool, and sweet, and dainty.

As she came in sight, their dusty and sweaty shirts

grew biting as the poisoned shirt of the Norse myth,
their bare feet in the brown dirt grew distressingly flat
and hoof-like, and their huge, dirty, brown, chapped
and swollen hands grew so repulsive that the mere
remote possibility of some time in the far future standing
a chance of having an introduction to her, caused them
to wipe their palms on their trousers' legs stealthily.

Lycurgus Banks swore when he saw Radbourn:
" That cuss thinks he's ol' hell this morning. He
don't earn his living. But he's just the kind of cuss
to get holt of all the purty girls."

Others gazed with simple, sad wistfulness upon
the slender figure, pale, sweet face, and dark eyes of
the young girl, feeling that to have talk with such a
fairylike creature was a happiness too great to ever
be their lot. And when she had passed they went
back to work with a sigh and feeling of loss.

As for Lily, she felt a pang of pity for these people.
She looked at this peculiar form of poverty and hard-
ship much as the fragile, tender girl of the city looks
upon the men laying a gas-main in the streets. She
felt, sympathetically, the heat and grime, and, though
but the faintest idea of what it meant to wear such
clothing came to her, she shuddered. Her eyes had
been opened to these things by Radbourn, a classmate
at the Seminary.

The young fellow knew that Lily was in love with
him, and made distinct effort to keep the talk upon
impersonal subjects. He liked her very much, probably because she listened so well.

"Poor fellows," sighed Lily, almost unconsciously, "I hate to see them working there in the dirt and hot sun. It seems a hopeless sort of life, doesn't it?"

"Oh, but this is the most beautiful part of the year," said Radbourn. "Think of them in the mud, in the sleet; think of them husking corn in the snow, a bitter wind blowing; think of them a month later in the harvest; think of them imprisoned here in winter!"

"Yes, it's dreadful! But I never felt it so keenly before. You have opened my eyes to it. Of course, I've been on a farm, but not to live there."

"Writers and orators have lied so long about 'the idyllic' in farm life, and said so much about the 'independent American farmer,' that he himself has remained blind to the fact that he's one of the hardest-working and poorest-paid men in America. See the houses they live in, — hovels."

"Yes, yes, I know," said Lily; a look of deeper pain swept over her face. "And the fate of the poor women; oh, the fate of the women!"

"Yes, it's a matter of statistics," went on Radbourn, pitilessly, "that the wives of the American farmers fill our insane asylums. See what a life they lead, most of them; no music, no books. Seventeen hours a day in a couple of small rooms — dens. Now there is Sim Burns! What a travesty of a home! Yet there are a dozen just as bad in sight. He works like a fiend — so does his wife — and what is their reward? Simply a hole to hibernate in and to sleep and eat in in summer. A dreary present and a well-nigh hopeless future. No, they have a future, if they knew it, and we must tell them."

"I know Mrs. Burns," Lily said, after a pause; "she sends several children to my school. Poor, pathetic little things, half-clad and wistful-eyed. They make my heart ache; they are so hungry for love, and so quick to learn."

As they passed the Burns farm, they looked for the wife, but she was not to be seen. The children had evidently gone up to the little white schoolhouse at the head of the lane. Radbourn let the reins fall slack as he talked on. He did not look at the girl; his eyebrows were drawn into a look of gloomy pain.

"It isn't so much the grime that I abhor, nor the labor that crooks their backs and makes their hands bludgeons. It's the horrible waste of life involved in it all. I don't believe God intended a man to be bent to plough-handles like that, but that isn't the worst of it. The worst of it is, these people live lives approaching automata. They become machines to serve others more lucky or more unscrupulous than themselves. What is the world of art, of music, of literature, to these poor devils, — to Sim Burns and his wife there, for example? Or even to the best of these farmers?"

The girl looked away over the shimmering lake of yellow-green corn. A choking came into her throat. Her gloved hand trembled.

"What is such a life worth? It's all very comfortable for us to say, 'They don't feel it.' How do we know what they feel? What do we know of their capacity for enjoyment of art and music? They never have leisure or opportunity. The master is very glad to be taught by preacher, and lawyer, and novelist, that his slaves are contented and never feel any longings for a higher life. These people live lives but little higher than their cattle — are *forced* to live so. Their hopes and aspirations are crushed out, their souls are twisted and deformed just as toil twists and deforms their bodies. They are on the same level as the city laborer. The very religion they hear is a soporific. They are taught to be content here that they may be happy hereafter. Suppose there isn't any hereafter ? "

" Oh, don't say that, please ! " Lily cried.

" But I don't *know* that there is," he went on remorselessly, " and I do know that these people are being robbed of something more than money, of all that makes life worth living. The promise of milk and honey in Canaan is all very well, but I prefer to have mine here; then I'm sure of it."

"What can we do ? " murmured the girl.

" Do ? Rouse these people for one thing; preach *discontent*, a noble discontent."

" It will only make them unhappy."

"No, it won't; not if you show them the way out. If it does, it's better to be unhappy striving for higher things, like a man, than to be content in a wallow like swine."

" But what *is* the way out ? "

This was sufficient to set Radbourn upon his hobbyhorse. He outlined his plan of action: the abolition of all indirect taxes, the State control of all privileges the private ownership of which interfered with the equal rights of all. He would utterly destroy speculative holdings of the earth. He would have land everywhere brought to its best use, by appropriating all ground rents to the use of the state, etc., etc., to which the girl listened with eager interest, but with only partial comprehension.

As they neared the little schoolhouse, a swarm of midgets in pink dresses, pink sun-bonnets, and brown legs, came rushing to meet their teacher, with that peculiar devotion the children in the country develop for a refined teacher.

Radbourn helped Lily out into the midst of the eager little scholars, who swarmed upon her like bees on a lump of sugar, till even Radbourn's gravity gave way, and he smiled into her lifted eyes, — an unusual smile, that strangely enough stopped the smile on her own lips, filling her face with a wistful shadow, and her breath came hard for a moment, and she trembled.

She loved that cold, stern face, oh, so much! and to have him smile was a pleasure that made her heart leap till she suffered a smothering pain. She turned to him to say : —

" I am very thankful, Mr. Radbourn, for another pleasant ride," adding in a lower tone, " it was a very great pleasure ; you always give me so much. I feel stronger and more hopeful."

" I'm glad you feel so. I was afraid I was prosy with my land doctrine."

" Oh, no ! Indeed no ! You have given me a new

hope; I am exalted with the thought; I shall try to think it all out and apply it."

And so they parted, the children looking on and slyly whispering among themselves. Radbourn looked back after a while, but the bare white hive had absorbed its little group, and was standing bleak as a tombstone and hot as a furnace on the naked plain in the blazing sun.

"America's pitiful boast!" said the young radical, looking back at it. "Only a miserable hint of what it might be."

All that forenoon, as Lily faced her noisy group of barefooted children, she was thinking of Radbourn, of his almost fierce sympathy for these poor, supine farmers, hopeless and in some cases content in their narrow lives. The children almost worshipped the beautiful girl who came to them as a revelation of exquisite neatness and taste, — whose very voice and intonation awed them.

They noted, unconsciously of course, every detail. Snowy linen, touches of soft color, graceful lines of bust and side, the slender fingers that could almost speak, so beautifully flexile were they. Lily herself sometimes, when she shook the calloused, knotted, stiffened hands of the women, shuddered with sympathetic pain to think that the crowning wonder and beauty of God's world should be so maimed and distorted from its true purpose.

Even in the children before her she could see the inherited results of fruitless labor, and, more pitiful yet,

in the bent shoulders of the older ones she could see the
beginnings of deformity that would soon be permanent;
and as these thoughts came to her, she clasped the
wondering children to her side, with a convulsive wish
to make life a little brighter for them.

"How is your mother to-day?" she asked of Sadie
Burns, as she was eating her luncheon on the drab-
colored table near the open window.

"Purty well," said Sadie, in a hesitating way.

Lily was looking out, and listening to the gophers
whistling as they raced to and fro. She could see Bob
Burns lying at length on the grass in the pasture over
the fence, his heels waving in the air, his hands holding
a string which formed a snare. It was like fishing to
young Izaak Walton.

It was very still and hot, and the cheep and trill of
the gophers and the chatter of the kingbirds alone broke
the silence. A cloud of butterflies were fluttering about
a pool near; a couple of big flies buzzed and mumbled
on the pane.

"What ails your mother?" Lily asked, recovering herself and looking at Sadie, who was distinctly ill at ease.

"Oh, I dunno," Sadie replied, putting one bare foot
across the other.

Lily insisted.

"She 'n' pa's had an awful row — "

"Sadie!" said the teacher, warningly, "what lan-
guage!"

"I mean they quarrelled, an' she don't speak to him
any more."

"Why, how dreadful!"

"An' pa, he's awful cross; and she won't eat when he does, an' I haf to wait on table."

"I believe I'll go down and see her this noon," said Lily to herself, as she divined a little of the state of affairs in the Burns family.

V

SIM was mending the pasture fence as Lily came down the road toward him. He had delayed going to dinner to finish his task, and was just about ready to go when Lily spoke to him.

"Good morning, Mr. Burns. I am just going down to see Mrs. Burns. It must be time to go to dinner, — aren't you ready to go? I want to talk with you."

Ordinarily he would have been delighted with the idea of walking down the road with the schoolma'am, but there was something in her look which seemed to tell him that she knew all about his trouble, and, besides, he was not in good humor.

"Yes, in a minnit — soon's I fix up this hole. Them shotes, I b'lieve, would go through a keyhole, if they could once get their snoots in."

He expanded on this idea as he nailed away, anxious to gain time. He foresaw trouble for himself. He couldn't be rude to this sweet and fragile girl. If a *man* had dared to attack him on his domestic shortcomings, he could have fought. The girl stood waiting for him, her large, steady eyes full of thought, gazing down at him from the shadow of her broad-brimmed hat.

"The world is so full of misery anyway, that we ought to do the best we can to make it less," she said at last, in a musing tone, as if her thoughts had unconsciously taken on speech. She had always appealed to him strongly, and never more so than in this softly uttered abstraction — that it was an abstraction added to its power with him.

He could find no words for reply, but picked up his hammer and nail-box, and slouched along the road by her side, listening without a word to her talk.

"Christ was patient, and bore with his enemies. Surely we ought to bear with our — friends," she went on, adapting her steps to his. He took off his torn straw hat and wiped his face on his sleeve, being much embarrassed and ashamed. Not knowing how to meet such argument, he kept silent.

"How *is* Mrs. Burns!" said Lily at length, determined to make him speak. The delicate meaning in the emphasis laid on *is* did not escape him.

"Oh, she's all right — I mean she's done her work jest the same as ever. I don't see her much — "

"I didn't know — I was afraid she was sick. Sadie said she was acting strangely."

"No, she's well enough — but — "

"But what is the trouble? Won't you let me help you, *won't* you?" she pleaded.

"Can't anybody help us. We've got 'o fight it out, I s'pose," he replied, a gloomy note of resentment creeping into his voice. "She's ben in a devil of a temper f'r a week."

"Haven't you been in the same kind of a temper too?" demanded Lily, firmly but kindly. "I think most troubles of this kind come from bad temper on both sides. Don't you? Have you done your share at being kind and patient?"

They had reached the gate now, and she laid her hand on his arm to stop him. He looked down at the slender gloved hand on his arm, feeling as if a giant had grasped him; then he raised his eyes to her face, flushing a purplish red as he remembered his grossness. It seemed monstrous in the presence of this girl-advocate. Her face was like silver; her eyes seemed pools of tears.

"I don't s'pose I have," he said at last, pushing by her. He could not have faced her glance another moment. His whole air conveyed the impression of destructive admission. Lily did not comprehend the extent of her advantage or she would have pursued it further. As it was she felt a little hurt as she entered the house. The table was set, but Mrs. Burns was nowhere to be seen. Calling her softly, the young girl passed through the shabby little living-room to the oven-like bedroom which opened off it, but no one was about. She stood for a moment shuddering at the wretchedness of the room.

Going back to the kitchen, she found Sim about beginning on his dinner. Little Pet was with him; the rest of the children were at the schoolhouse.

"Where is she?"

"I d' know. Out in the garden, I expect. She
don't eat with me now. I never see her. She don't
come near *me*. I ain't seen her since Saturday."

Lily was shocked inexpressibly and began to see more
clearly the magnitude of the task she had set herself to
do. But it must be done; she felt that a tragedy was
not far off. It must be averted.

" Mr. Burns, what have you done? What *have* you
done?" she asked in terror and horror.

" Don't lay it all to *me!* She hain't done nawthin'
but complain f'r ten years. I couldn't do nothin' to
suit her. She was always naggin' me."

"I don't think Lucretia Burns would nag anybody.
I don't say you're *all* to blame, but I'm afraid you
haven't acknowledged you were *any* to blame. I'm
afraid you've not been patient with her. I'm going out
to bring her in. If she comes, will you *say* you were
part to blame? You needn't beg her pardon — just say
you'll try to be better. Will you do it? Think how
much she has done for you! Will you?"

He remained silent, and looked discouragingly rude.
His sweaty, dirty shirt was open at the neck, his arms
were bare, his scraggly teeth were yellow with tobacco,
and his uncombed hair lay tumbled about on his high,
narrow head. His clumsy, unsteady hands played with
the dishes on the table. His pride was struggling with
his sense of justice; he knew he ought to consent, and
yet it was so hard to acknowledge himself to blame.
The girl went on in a voice piercingly sweet, trembling
with pity and pleading.

I

"What word can I carry to her from you? I'm going to go and see her. If I could take a word from *you*, I know she would come back to the table. Shall I tell her you feel to blame?"

The answer was a long time coming; at last the man nodded an assent, the sweat pouring from his purple face. She had set him thinking; her victory was sure.

Lily almost ran out into the garden and to the strawberry patch, where she found Lucretia in her familiar, colorless, shapeless dress, picking berries in the hot sun, the mosquitoes biting her neck and hands.

"Poor, pathetic, dumb sufferer!" the girl thought as she ran up to her.

She dropped her dish as she heard Lily coming, and gazed up into the tender, pitying face. Not a word was spoken, but something she saw there made her eyes fill with tears, and her throat swell. It was pure sympathy. She put her arms around the girl's neck and sobbed for the first time since Friday night. Then they sat down on the grass under the hedge, and she told her story, interspersed with Lily's horrified comments.

When it was all told, the girl still sat listening. She heard Radbourn's calm, slow voice again. It helped her not to hate Burns; it helped her to pity and understand him.

"You must remember that such toil brutalizes a man; it makes him callous, selfish, unfeeling, necessarily. A fine nature must either adapt itself to its hard surroundings or die. Men who toil terribly in filthy garments day after day and year after year cannot easily keep gentle; the frost and grime, the heat and cold, will soon or late enter into their souls. The case is not all in favor of the suffering wives and against the brutal husbands. If the farmer's wife is dulled and crazed by her routine, the farmer himself is degraded and brutalized."

As well as she could Lily explained all this to the woman, who lay with her face buried in the girl's lap. Lily's arms were about her thin shoulders in an agony of pity.

" It's hard, Lucretia, I know, — more than you can bear, — but you mustn't forget what Sim endures too. He goes out in the storms and in the heat and dust. His boots are hard, and see how his hands are all bruised and broken by his work! He was tired and hungry when he said that — he didn't really mean it."

The wife remained silent.

" Mr. Radbourn says work, as things go now, *does* degrade a man in spite of himself. He says men get coarse and violent in spite of themselves, just as women do when everything goes wrong in the house, — when the flies are thick, and the fire won't burn, and the irons stick to the clothes. You see, you both suffer. Don't lay up this fit of temper against Sim — will you ? "

The wife lifted her head and looked away. Her face was full of hopeless weariness.

" It ain't this once. It ain't that 't all. It's having no let-up. Just goin' the same thing right over 'n' over — no hope of anything better."

" If you had hope of another world — "

" Don't talk that. I don't want that kind o' comfert.

I want a decent chance here. I want 'o rest an' be happy *now*." Lily's big eyes were streaming with tears. What should she say to the desperate woman? "What's the use? We might jest as well die — all of us."

The woman's livid face appalled the girl. She was gaunt, heavy-eyed, nerveless. Her faded dress settled down over her limbs, showing the swollen knees and thin calves; her hands, with distorted joints, protruded painfully from her sleeves. All about her was the ever recurring wealth and cheer of nature that knows no favor, — the bees and flies buzzing in the sun, the jay and the kingbird in the poplars, the smell of strawberries, the motion of lush grass, the shimmer of cornblades tossed gayly as banners in a conquering army.

Like a flash of keener light, a sentence shot across the girl's mind: "Nature knows no title-deed. The bounty of her mighty hands falls as the sunlight falls, copious, impartial; her seas carry all ships; her air is for all lips, her lands for all feet."

"Poverty and suffering such as yours will not last." There was something in the girl's voice that roused the woman. She turned her dull eyes upon the youthful face.

Lily took her hand in both hers as if by a caress she could impart her own faith.

"Look up, dear. When nature is so good and generous, man must come to be better, surely. Come, go in the house again. Sim is there; he expects you; he told me to tell you he was sorry." Lucretia's face twitched a little at that, but her head was bent. "Come; you can't live this way. There isn't any other place to go to."

No, that was the bitterest truth. Where on this wide earth, with its forth-shooting fruits and grains, its fragrant lands and shining seas, could this dwarfed, bent, broken, middle-aged woman go? Nobody wanted her, nobody cared for her. But the wind kissed her drawn lips as readily as those of the girl, and the blooms of clover nodded to her as if to a queen.

Lily had said all she could. Her heart ached with unspeakable pity and a sort of terror.

"Don't give up, Lucretia. This may be the worst hour of your life. Live and bear with it all for Christ's sake, — for your children's sake. Sim told me to tell you he was to blame. If you will only see that you are both to blame and yet neither to blame, then you can rise above it. Try, dear!"

Something that was in the girl imparted itself to the wife, electrically. She pulled herself together, rose silently, and started toward the house. Her face was rigid, but no longer sullen. Lily followed her slowly, wonderingly.

As she neared the kitchen door, she saw Sim still sitting at the table; his face was unusually grave and soft. She saw him start and shove back his chair, saw Lucretia go to the stove and lift the tea-pot, and heard her say, as she took her seat beside the baby : —

"Want some more tea?"

She had become a wife and mother again, but in what spirit the puzzled girl could not say.

LOGAN AT PEACH TREE CREEK

A VETERAN'S STORY

You know that day at Peach Tree Creek,
When the Rebs with their circling, scorching wall
Of smoke-hid cannon and sweep of flame
Drove in our flanks, back! back! and all
Our toil seemed lost in the storm of shell? —
That desperate day McPherson fell!

Our regiment stood in a little glade
Set round with half-grown red-oak trees;
An awful place to stand, in full fair sight,
While the minie bullets hummed like bees,
And comrades dropped on either side —
That fearful day McPherson died!

The roar of the battle, steady, stern,
Rung in our ears.   Upon our eyes
The belching cannon smoke, the half-hid swing
Of deploying troops, the groans, the cries,
The hoarse commands, the sickening smell —
That blood-red day McPherson fell!

But we stood there, — when out from the trees,
Out of the smoke and dismay, to the right
Burst a rider, — his head was bare, his eye
Had a blaze like a lion fain for fight;
His long hair, black as the deepest night,
Streamed out on the wind.   And the might
Of his plunging horse was a tale to tell,

And his voice rang high like a bugle's swell;
" Men, the enemy hem us on every side;
We'll whip 'em yet!   Close up that breach —
Remember your flag — don't give an inch!
The right flank's gaining and soon will reach —
Forward, boys, and give 'em hell!"
Said Logan, after McPherson fell.

We laughed and cheered and the red ground shook,
As the general plunged along the line
Through the deadliest rain of screaming shells;
For the sound of his voice refreshed us all,
And we filled the gap like a roaring tide,
And saved the day McPherson died!

And that was twenty years ago,
And part of a horrible dream now past.
For Logan, the lion, the drums throb low,
And the flag swings low on the mast.
He has followed his mighty chieftain through
The mist-hung stream, where gray and blue
One color stands,
And North to South extends the hand.
It's right that deeds of war and blood
Should be forgot, but, spite of all,
I think of Logan now, as he rode
That day across the field; I hear the call
Of his trumpet voice, see the battle shine
In his stern, black eyes, and down the line
Of cheering men, I see him ride,
As on the day McPherson died!

SOME VILLAGE CRONIES

SOME VILLAGE CRONIES

COLONEL PEAVY had just begun the rubber with Squire Gordon, of Cerro Gordo County. They were seated in Robie's grocery, behind the rusty old cannon stove, the checker-board spread out on their knees. The Colonel was grinning in great glee, wringing his bony yellow hands in nervous excitement, in strong contrast to the stolid calm of the fat Squire.

The Colonel had won the last game by a large margin, and was sure he had his opponent's dodges well in hand. It was early in the evening, and the grocery was comparatively empty. Robie was figuring at a desk, and old Judge Brown stood in legal gravity warming his legs at the red-hot stove, and swaying gently back and forth in speechless content. It was a tough night outside, one of the toughest for years. The frost had completely shut the window-panes as with thick blankets of snow. The streets were silent.

"I don't know," said the Judge, reflectively, to Robie, breaking the silence in his rasping, judicial bass, "I don't know as there has been such a night as this since the night of February 2, '59; that was the night James Kirk went under — Honorable Kirk, you remember — knew him well. Brilliant fellow, ornament to Western bar. But whiskey downed him. It'll beat the oldest man — I wonder where the boys

123

all are to-night? Don't seem to be any one stirring on the street. Aren't frightened out by the cold?"

"Shouldn't wonder." Robie was busy at his desk, and not in humor for conversation on reminiscent lines. The two old war dogs at the board had settled down to one of those long, silent struggles which ensue when two champions meet. In the silence which followed, the Judge was looking attentively at the back of the Colonel, and thinking that the old thief was getting about down to skin and bone. He turned with a yawn to Robie, saying : —

"This cold weather must take hold of the old Colonel terribly, he's so damnably thin and bald, you know, — bald as a babe. The fact is, the old Colonel ain't long for this world, anyway; think so, Hank?" Robie making no reply, the Judge relapsed into silence for a while, watching the cat (perilously walking along the edge of the upper shelf) and listening to the occasional hurrying footsteps outside. "I don't know *when* I've seen the windows closed up so, Hank; go down to thirty below to-night; devilish strong wind blowing, too; tough night on the prairies, Hank."

"You bet," replied Hank, briefly.

The Colonel was plainly getting excited. His razorlike back curved sharper than ever as he peered into the intricacies of the board to spy the trap which the fat Squire had set for him. At this point the squeal of boots on the icy walk outside paused, and a moment later Amos Ridings entered, with whiskers covered with ice, and looking like a huge bear in his buffalo coat.

" By Josephus! it's cold," he roared, as he took off his gloves and began to warm his face and hands at the fire.

" Is it ? " asked the Judge, comfortably, rising on his tiptoes, only to fall back into his usual attitude legal, legs well spread, shoulders thrown back.

" You bet it is! " replied Amos. "I d' know when I've felt the cold more'n I have t'-day. It's jest snifty; doubles me up like a jack-knife, Judge. How do you stand it ? "

" Toler'ble, toler'ble, Amos. But we're agin', we're not what we were once. Cold takes hold of us."

" That's a fact," answered Amos to the retrospective musings of the Judge. " Time was you an' me would go t' singing-school or sleigh-riding with the girls on a night like this and never notice it."

" Yes, sir; yes, sir ! " said the Judge with a sigh. It was a little uncertain in Robie's mind whether the Judge was regretting the lost ability to stand the cold, or the lost pleasure of riding with the girls.

" Great days, those, gentlemen ! Lived in Vermont then. Hot-blooded — lungs like an ox. I remember, Sallie Dearborn and I used to go a-foot to singing-school down the valley four miles. But now, wouldn't go riding to-night with the handsomest woman in America, and the best cutter in Rock River."

" Oh! you've got both feet in the grave up t' the ankles, anyway," said Robie, from his desk; but the Judge immovably gazed at the upper shelf on the other side of the room, where the boilers and pans and washboards were stored.

"The Judge is a little on the sentimental order to-night," said Amos.

"Hold on, Colonel! hold on. You've *got* 'o jump. Hah! hah!" roared Gordon from the checker-board. "That's right, that's right!" he ended, as the Colonel complied reluctantly.

"Sock it to the old cuss!" commented Amos. "What I was going to say," he resumed, rolling down the collar of his coat, "was, that when my wife helped me bundle up t'-night, she said I was gitt'n' t' be an old granny. We *are* agin', Judge, the's no denyin' that. We're both gray as Norway rats now. An' speaking of us agin' reminds me — have y' noticed how bald the old Kyernel's gitt'n'?"

"I have, Amos," answered the Judge, mournfully. "The old man's head is showing age, showing age! Getting thin up there, very thin."

The old Colonel bent to his work with studied abstraction, and even when Amos said, judicially, after long scrutiny, "Yes, he'll soon be as bald as a plate," he only lifted one yellow, freckled, bony hand, and brushed his carroty growth of hair across the spot under discussion. Gordon's fat paunch shook in silent laughter, nearly displacing the board.

"I was just telling Robie," pursued Brown, still retaining his reminiscent intonation, "that this storm takes the cake over anything — "

At this point Steve Roach and another fellow entered. Steve was Ridings's hired hand, a herculean fellow, with a drawl, and a liability for taking offence quite as remarkable.

"Say! gents, I'm no spring rooster, but this jest gits away with anything in the line of cold *I* ever see."

While this communication was being received in ruminative silence, Steve was holding his ears in his hand and gazing at the intent champions at the board. There they sat; the old Squire panting and wheezing in his excitement, for he was planning a great "snap" on the Colonel, whose red and freckled nose almost touched the board. It was a solemn battle hour. The wind howled mournfully outside, the timbers of the store creaked in the cold, and the huge cannon stove roared in steady bass.

"Speaking about ears," said Steve, after a silence, "dummed if I'd like t' be quite s' bare 'round the ears as Kernel there. I wonder if any o' you fellers has noticed how the ol' feller's lost hair this last summer. He's gittin' bald, they's no coverin' it up, — gittin' bald as a plate."

"You're right, Stephen," said the Judge, as he gravely took his stand behind his brother advocate and studied, with the eye of an adept, the field of battle. "We were noticing it when you came in. It's a sad thing, but it must be admitted."

"It's the Kyernel's brains wearin' up through his hair, I take it," commented Amos, as he helped himself to a handful of peanuts out of the bag behind the counter. "Say, Steve, did y' stuff up that hole in front of ol' Barney?"

A shout was heard outside, and then a rush against the door, and immediately two young fellows burst in, followed by a fierce gust of snow. One was Professor Knapp, the other Editor Foster, of the *Morning Call*.

" Well, gents, how's this for high ? " said Foster, in a peculiar tone of voice, at which all began to smile. He was a slender fellow with close-clipped, assertive red hair. " In this company we now have the majesty of the law, the power of the press, and the underpinning of the American civilization all represented. Hello ! There are a couple of old roosters with their heads together. Gordon, my old enemy, how are you ? "

Gordon waved him off with a smile and a wheeze. " Don't bother me now. I've got 'im. I'm laying f'r the old dog. Whist ! "

" Got nothing ! " snarled the Colonel. " You try that on if you want to. Just swing that man in there if you think it's healthy for him. Just as like as not, you'll slip up on that little trick."

" Ha ! Say you so, old True Penny ? The Kunnel has met a foeman worthy of his steel," said Foster, in great glee, as he bent above the Colonel. " I know. *How* do I know, quotha ? By the curve on the Kunnel's back. The size of the parabola described by that backbone accurately gauges his adversary's skill. But, by the way, gentlemen, have you — but that's a nice point, and I refer all nice points to Professor Knapp. Professor, is it in good taste to make remarks concerning the dress or features of another ? "

" Certainly not," answered Knapp, a handsome young fellow with a yellow mustache.

" Not when the person is an esteemed public character, like the Colonel here? What I was about to remark, if it had been proper, was that the old fellow is getting wofully bald. He'll soon be bald as an egg."

"Say!" asked the Colonel, "I want to know how long you're going to keep this thing up? Somebody's dummed sure t' get hurt soon."

"There, there, Colonel," said Brown, soothingly, "don't get excited; you'll lose the rubber. Don't mind 'em. Keep cool."

"Yes, keep cool, Kunnel; it's only our solicitude for your welfare," chipped in Foster. Then, addressing the crowd in a general sort of way, he speculated: "Curious how a man, a plain American citizen like Colonel Peavy, wins a place in the innermost affections of a whole people."

"That's so!" murmured the rest.

"He can't grow bald without deep sympathy from his fellow-citizens. It amounts to a public calamity."

The old Colonel glared in speechless wrath.

"Say, gents," pleaded Gordon, "let up on the old man for the present. He's going to need all of himself if he gets out o' the trap he's in now." He waved his fat hand over the Colonel's head, and smiled blandly at the crowd hugging the stove.

"My head may be bald," grated the old man, with a death's-head grin indescribably ferocious, "but it's got brains enough in it to skunk any man in this crowd three games out o' five."

"The ol' man rather gits the laugh on y' there, gents," called Robie from the other side of the counter.

K

"I hain't seen the old skeesix play better'n he did last night, in years."

"Not since his return from Canada, after the war, I reckon," said Amos, from the kerosene barrel.

"Hold on, Amos," put in the Judge, warningly, "that's outlawed. Talking about being bald and the war reminds me of the night Walters and I — by the way, where is Walters to-night?"

"Sick," put in the Colonel, straightening up exultantly. "I waxed him three straight games last night. You won't see him again till spring. Skunked him once, and beat him twice."

"Oh, git out."

"Hear the old seed twitter!"

"Did you ever notice, gentlemen, how lying and baldness go together?" queried Foster, reflectively.

"No! Do they?"

"Invariably. I've known many colossal liars, and they were all as bald as apples."

The Colonel was getting nervous, and was so slow that even Gordon (who could sit and stare at the board a full half-hour without moving) began to be impatient.

"Come, Colonel, marshal your forces a little more promptly. If you're going at me *échelon*, sound y'r bugle; I'm ready."

"Don't worry," answered the Colonel, in his calmest nasal. "I'll accommodate you with all the fight you want."

"Did it ever occur to you," began the Judge again, addressing the crowd generally, as he moved back to the stove and lit another cigar, " did it ever occur to you that it is a little singular a man should get bald on the *top* of his head first ? Curious fact. So accustomed to it we no longer wonder at it. Now see the Colonel there ; quite a growth of hair on his clapboarding, as it were, but devilish thin on his roof."

Here the Colonel looked up and tried to say something, but the Judge went on imperturbably : —

" Now, I take it that it's strictly providential that a man gets bald on top of his head first, because if he *must* get bald, it is best to get bald where it can be covered up."

" By jinks, that's a fact ! " said Foster, in high admiration of the Judge's ratiocination. Steve was specially pleased, and, drawing a neck-yoke from a barrel standing near, pounded the floor vigorously.

" Talking about being bald," put in Foster, " reminds me of a scheme of mine, which is to send no one out to fight Indians but bald men. Think how powerless they'd be in — "

The talk now drifted off to Indians, politics, and religion, edged round to the war, when the grave Judge began telling Ridings and Robie just how " Kilpatrick charged along the Granny White Turnpike," and, on a sheet of wrapping paper, was showing where Major John Dilrigg fell. " I was on his left, about thirty yards, when I saw him throw up his hand — "

Foster in a low voice was telling something to the Professor and two or three others, which made them whoop with uncontrollable merriment, when the roar-

ing voice of big Sam Walters was heard outside, and a
moment later he rolled into the room, filling it with his
noise. Lottridge, the watchmaker, and Erlberg, the
German baker, came in with him.

"*Hello*, hello, *hello!*   All here, are yeh?"

"All here waiting for you — and the turnkey," said
Foster.

"Well, here I am. Always on hand, like a sore
thumb in huskin' season. What's goin' on here? A
game, hey? Hello, Gordon, it's you, is it? Colonel,
I owe you several for last night; but what the devil
yo' got your cap on fur, Colonel? Ain't it warm
enough here for yeh?"

The desperate Colonel, who had snatched up his cap
when he heard Walters coming, grinned painfully, pulling his straggly red and white beard nervously. The
strain was beginning to tell on his iron nerves. He
removed the cap, and with a few muttered words went
back to the game, but there was a dangerous gleam in
his fishy blue eyes, and the grizzled tufts of red hair
above his eyes lowered threateningly. A man who is
getting swamped in a game of checkers is not in a mood
to bear pleasantly any remarks on his bald head.

"Oh! don't take it off, Colonel," went on his tormentor, hospitably. "When a man gets as old as you
are, he's privileged to wear his cap. I wonder if any
of you fellers have noticed how the Colonel is shedding
his hair."

The old man leaped up, scattering the men on the
checker-board, which flew up and struck Squire Gordon

in the face, knocking him off his stool. The old Colonel was ashy pale, and his eyes glared out from under his huge brow like sapphires lit by flame. His spare form, clothed in a seedy Prince Albert frock, towered with a singular dignity. His features worked convulsively a moment, then he burst forth like the explosion of a safety valve: —

"Shuttup, damyeh!"

And then the crowd whooped, roared, and rolled on the counters and barrels, and roared and whooped again. They stamped and yelled, and ran around like fiends, kicking the boxes and banging the coal-scuttle in a perfect pandemonium of mirth, leaving the old man standing there helpless in his wrath, mad enough to shoot. Steve was just preparing to seize the old man from behind, when Squire Gordon, struggling to his feet among the spittoons, cried out, in the voice of a colonel of Fourth of July militia: —

"H-O-L-D!"

Silence was restored, and all stood around in expectant attitudes to hear the Squire's explanation. He squared his elbows, shoved up his sleeves, puffed out his fat cheeks, moistened his lips, and began pompously: —

"Gentlemen —"

"You've hit it; that's us," said some of the crowd in applause.

"Gentlemen of Rock River, when, in the course of human events, rumor had blow'd to my ears the history of the checker-playing of Rock River, and when I had waxed Cerro Gordo, and Claiborne, and Mower, then, when I say to my ears was borne the clash of resounding arms in Rock River, the emporium of Rock County, then did I yearn for more worlds to conquer, and behold, I buckled on my armor and I am here."

"Behold, he is here," said Foster, in confirmation of the statement. "Good for you, Squire; git breath and go for us some more."

"Hurrah for the Squire," etc.

"I came seekin' whom I might devour, like a raging lion. I sought foeman worthy of my steel. I leaped into the arena and blew my challenge to the four quarters of Rock — "

"Good f'r you! Settemupagin! Go it, you old balloon," they all applauded.

"Knowing my prowess, I sought a fair fout and no favors. I met the enemy, and he was mine. Champion after champion went down before me like — went down like — ahem! went *down* before me like grass before the mighty cyclone of the Andes."

"Listen to the old blowhard," said Steve.

"Put him out," said the speaker, imperturbably. "Gentlemen, have I the floor?"

"You have," replied Brown, "but come to the point. The Colonel is anxious to begin shooting." The Colonel, who began to suspect himself victimized, stood wondering what under heaven they were going to do next.

"I am a-gitt'n' there," said the orator, with a broad and sunny condescension. "I found your champions an' laid 'em low. I waxed Walters, and then I tackled the Colonel. I tried the *échelon*, the 'general advance,'

then the 'give away' and 'flank' movements. But
the Colonel *was there!* Till this last game it was a
fair field and no favor. And now, gentlemen of Rock,
I desire t' state to my deeply respected opponent that
he is still champion of Rock, and I'm not sure but of
Northern Iowa."

"Three cheers for the Kunnel!"

And while they were being given the Colonel's brows
relaxed, and the champion of Cerro Gordo continued
earnestly : —

"And now I wish to state to Colonel the solemn
fact that I had nothing to do with the job put up on
him to-night. I scorn to use such means in a battle.
Colonel, you may be as bald as an apple, or an egg,
yes, or a *plate*, but you can play more checkers than
any man I ever met; more checkers than any other
man on God's green footstool — with one single, lone
exception, — myself."

At this moment, somebody hit the Squire from Cerro
Gordo with a decayed apple, and as the crowd shouted
and groaned, Robie turned down the lights on the tumult.
The old Colonel seized the opportunity for putting a
handful of salt down Walters's neck, and slipped out
of the door like a ghost. As the crowd swarmed out
on the icy walk, Editor Foster yelled : —

"Gents! let me give you a pointer. Keep your eye
peeled for the next edition of the Rock River *Morning
Call*."

And the bitter wind swept away the answering
shouts of the pitiless gang.

THE WAR OF RACE

SMALL men for golden hire and fame
Go out against the Redman on the sand;
They go with sneers and curses at his name.
He meets them with an open hand,
And sadly asks them why they come;
They answer " By command of might,
Move on, or we will beat the drum,
And you shall answer for the fight."

Then the Redman's face grows dark,
With sombre eyes he sits at prayer;
" O Tirawa!   Where shall thy children go?   Hark
To our voices you who live in air."
There comes no answer to his wailing call,
Then booms the sullen war drum, upon the air,
The cries of woful women lift and fall,
And on fierce lips the council fires flare.

DRIFTING CRANE

DRIFTING CRANE

THE people of Boomtown invariably spoke of Henry Wilson as the oldest settler in the Jim Valley, as he was of Buster County, but the Eastern man, with his ideas of an "old settler," was surprised as he met the short, silent, middle-aged man, who was very loath to tell anything about himself, and about whom many strange and thrilling stories were told by good story-tellers. In 1879 he was the only settler in the upper part of the valley, living alone on the banks of the Elm, a slow, tortuous stream pulsing lazily down the valley, too small to be called a river and too long to be called a creek. For two years, it is said, Wilson had only the company of his cattle, especially during the winter-time, and now and then a visit from an Indian, or a trapper after mink and musk-rats.

Between his ranch and the settlements in Eastern Dakota there was the wedge-shaped reservation known as the Sisseton Indian Reserve, on which were stationed the customary agency and company of soldiers. But, of course, at that time the Indians were not restricted closely to the bounds of the reserve, but ranged freely over the vast and beautiful prairie lying between the coteaux or ranges of low hills which mark out "the Jim Valley." The valley was unsurveyed for the most part, and the Indians naturally felt a sort of proprietorship in it, and when Wilson drove his cattle down into the valley and squatted, the chief, Drifting Crane, welcomed him, as a host might, to an abundant feast whose hospitality was presumed upon, but who felt the need of sustaining his reputation for generosity, and submitted graciously.

The Indians during the first summer got to know Wilson, and liked him for his silence, his courage, his simplicity; but the older men pondered upon the matter a great deal and watched with grave faces to see him ploughing up the sod for his garden. There was something strange in this solitary man thus deserting his kindred, coming here to live alone with his cattle; they could not understand it. What they said in those pathetic, dimly lighted lodges will never be known; but when winter came, and the new-comer did not drive his cattle back over the hills as they thought he would, then the old chieftains took long counsel upon it. Night after night they smoked upon it, and at last Drifting Crane said to two of his young men: "Go ask this cattleman why he remains in the cold and snow with his cattle. Ask him why he does not drive his cattle home."

This was in March, and one evening a couple of days later, as Wilson was about reëntering his shanty at the close of his day's work, he was confronted by two stalwart Indians, who greeted him pleasantly.

"How d'e do? How d'e do?" he said in reply. "Come in. Come in and take a snack."

The Indians entered and sat silently while he put

grasses for stock. It spoke of the successful venture of
the lonely settler Wilson, how his stock fattened upon
the winter grasses without shelter, etc., what vegetables
he grew, etc., etc.

Wilson was reading this paper for the sixth time one
evening in May. He had laid off his boots, his pipe
was freshly filled, and he sat in the doorway in vast
content, unmindful of the glory of color that filled
the western sky, and the superb evening chorus of the
prairie-chickens, holding conventions on every hillock.
He felt something touch him on the shoulder, and
looked up to see a tall Indian gazing down upon him
with a look of strange pride and gravity. Wilson
sprang to his feet and held out his hand.

"Drifting Crane, how d'e do?"

The Indian bowed, but did not take the settler's
hand. Drifting Crane would have been called old if
he had been a white man, and there was a look of age
in the fixed lines of his powerful, strongly modelled face,
but no suspicion of weakness in the splendid poise of his
broad, muscular body. There was a smileless gravity
about his lips and eyes which was very impressive.

"I'm glad to see you. Come in and get something
to eat," said Wilson, after a moment's pause.

The chief entered the cabin and took a seat near the
door. He took a cup of milk and some meat and bread
silently, and ate while listening to the talk of the
settler.

"I don't brag on my biscuits, chief, but they *eat*, if
a man is hungry. An' the milk's all right. I suppose

you've come to see why I ain't moseying back over the divide ? "

The chief, after a long pause, began to speak in a low, slow voice, as if choosing his words. He spoke in broken English, of course, but his speech was very direct and plain, and had none of these absurd figures of rhetoric which romancers invariably put into the mouths of Indians. His voice was almost lionlike in its depth, and yet was not unpleasant. It was easy to see that he was a chief by virtue of his own personality.

"Cattleman, my young men brought me bad message from you. They brought your words to me, saying, he will not go away."

"That's about the way the thing stands," replied Wilson, in response to the question that was in the old chief's steady eyes. "I'm here to stay. This ain't your land; this is Uncle Sam's land, and part of it'll be mine as soon as the surveyors come to measure it off."

"Who gave it away ? " asked the chief. "My people were cheated out of it ; they didn't know what they were doing."

"I can't help that ; that's for Congress to say. That's the business of the Great Father at Washington." Wilson's voice changed. He knew and liked the chief ; he didn't want to offend him. "They ain't no use making a fuss, chief. You won't gain anything."

There was a look of deep sorrow in the old man's face. At last he spoke again: "The cattleman is welcome; but he must go, because whenever one white man goes and calls it good, the others come. Drifting Crane has seen it far in the east twice. The white men come thick as the grass. They tear up the sod. They build houses. They scare the buffalo away. They spoil my young men with whiskey. Already they begin to climb the eastern hills. Soon they will fill the valley, and Drifting Crane and his people will be surrounded. The sod will all be black."

"I hope you're right," was the rancher's grim reply.

"But they will not come if the cattleman go back to say the water is not good, there is no grass, and the Indians own the land."

Wilson smiled at the childish faith of the chief. "Won't do, chief — won't do. That won't do any good. I might as well stay."

The chief rose. He was touched by the settler's laugh; his eyes flashed; his voice took on a sterner note. "The white man *must* go!"

Wilson rose also. He was not a large man, but he was a very resolute one. "I shan't go," he said through his clenched teeth. Each man understood the tones of the other perfectly.

It was a thrilling, a significant scene. It was in absolute truth the meeting of the modern vidette of civilization with one of the rear-guard of retreating barbarism. Each man was a type; each was wrong, and each was right. The Indian as true and noble from the barbaric point of view as the white man. He was a warrior and hunter; made so by circumstances over which he had

L

no control. Guiltless as the panther, because war to a savage is the necessity of life.

The settler represented the unflagging energy and fearless heart of the American pioneer. Narrow-minded, partly brutalized by hard labor and a lonely life, yet an admirable figure for all that. As he looked into the Indian's face he seemed to grow in height. He felt behind him all the weight of the millions of westward moving settlers; he stood the representative of an unborn State. He took down a rifle from the wall, the magazine rifle, most modern of guns; he patted the stock, pulled the crank, throwing a shell into view.

" You know this thing, chief ? "

The Indian nodded slightly.

" Well, I'll go when — this — is — empty."

" But my young men are many."

" So are the white men — my brothers."

The chief's head dropped forward. Wilson, ashamed of his boasting, put the rifle back on the wall.

" I'm not here to fight. You can kill me any time. You could 'a' killed me to-night, but it wouldn't do any good. It 'ud only make it worse for you. Why, they'll be a town in here bigger'n all your tribe before two grass from now. It ain't no use, Drifting Crane; it's *got* to be. You an' I can't help n'r hinder it. I know just how you feel about it, but I tell yeh it ain't no use to fight."

Drifting Crane turned his head and gazed out on the western sky, still red with the light of the fallen sun. His face was rigid as bronze, but there was a dreaming, prophetic look in his eyes. A lump came into the settler's throat; for the first time in his life he got a glimpse of the infinite despair of the Indian. He forgot that Drifting Crane was the representative of a " vagabond race "; he saw in him, or rather *felt* in him, something almost magnetic. He was a *man*, and a man of sorrows. The settler's voice was husky when he spoke again, and his lips trembled.

" Chief, I'd go to-morrow if it 'ud do any good, but it won't — not a particle. You know that when you stop to think a minute. What good did it do to massa*cree* all them settlers at New Ulm? What good will it do to murder me and a hundred others? Not a bit. A thousand others would take our places. So I might just as well stay, and we might just as well keep good friends. Killin' is out o' fashion; don't do any good."

There was a twitching about the stern mouth of the Indian chief. He understood all too well the irresistible logic of the pioneer. He kept his martial attitude, but his broad chest heaved painfully, and his eyes grew dim. At last he said, " Good-by. Cattleman right; Drifting Crane wrong. Shake hands. Good-by." He turned and strode away.

The rancher watched him till he mounted his pony, picketed down by the river; watched him as, with drooping head and rein flung loose upon the neck of his horse, he rode away into the dusk, hungry, weary, and despairing, to face his problem alone. Again, for the thousandth time, the impotence of the Indian's arm and the hopelessness of his fate were shown as perfectly as if two armies had met and soaked the beautiful prairie sod with blood.

" This is all wrong," muttered the settler. " There's land enough for us all, or ought to be. I don't understand — Well, I'll leave it to Uncle Sam, anyway." He ended with a sigh.

PAID HIS WAY

No, Steve, I ain't complainin' any,
I'll go, — if y' think it's right;
I don't ask a single bite n'r a penny,
More n'r less 'n jest what's white —
But son, bime-by, when the old man's done for,
Jest remember my words to-day;
Y' don't like to have me round h'yere,
But I reckon I've paid m' way.

I was eighty-one last January, —
Born in the Buckeye State,
I've opened two farms on the prairie,
An' worked on 'em early and late.
Come rain or come shine, a scrapin' t' earn
Every mouthful we eat, an' I want 'o say,
That I never rode in no *free* concern
That I didn't pay my way.

Y'r mother and me worked mighty hard,
How hard you'll never know;
In cold and heat a-standin' guard
To keep off the rain and snow.
The mortgige kep' eating in nearer to bone,
And the war it come along too,
But I went — left mother alone
With Sis in the cradle — and you.

Served my time, an' commenced agin
On an Ioway prairie quarter,

An' there I ploughed an' sowed an' fenced,
And *nigged* as no human orter,
To raise you young ones and feed m' wife —
Y'r mother scrimped and scrubbed till her hair was
    gray,
And I reckon we paid our way.

No, y'r high-toned tavern *ain't* good enough
F'r a man like me to die in !
The work that's made me crooked and rough
Should 'a' earned me a bed to lie in
Under the roof of my only son, —
If his wife is proud an' gay ;
For I boosted y' into the place y've won.
O I reckon I've paid my way.

Y'r wife I know is turrible set,
She's mighty hansom to see
I'll admit, but it's a turrible fret
This havin' to eat with me.
She never speaks, and she never seems
To be listnin' to what I say,
But the children do, *they* don't know yet,
Their grandad's in the way.

I d' know's you're *very* much to blame
For wantin' to have me go,
But, Steve, I'm glad y'r mother's dead,
'Twould break her heart to know.

She'd say I orter live here,
What time I've got to stay,
For, Stephen, I've travelled for fifty years,
An' I've always paid my way.

I aint' a-goin' to bother y' long,
I'll be a-pioneerin' further West
Where mother is, and God'll say,
Take it easy, Amos, y've earned a rest —
So, Stevie, I want to stay with you,
I want 'o *work* while I stay,
Jes' give me a little sumpin' to do,
I reckon I'll pay my way.

DADDY DEERING

DADDY DEERING

I

THEY were threshing on Farmer Jennings's place
when Daddy made his very characteristic appearance.
Milton, a boy of thirteen, was gloomily holding sacks
for the measurer, and the glory of the October day was
dimmed by the suffocating dust, and poisoned by the
smarting beards and chaff which had worked their way
down his neck. The bitterness of the dreaded task was
deepened also by contrast with the gambols of his cousin
Billy, who was hunting rats with Growler amid the last
sheaves of the stack bottom. The piercing shrieks of
Billy, as he clapped his hands in murderous glee, mingled
now and again with the barking of the dog.

The machine seemed to fill the world with its snarling boom, which became a deafening yell when the
cylinder ran empty for a moment. It was nearly noon,
and the men were working silently, with occasional
glances toward the sun to see how near dinner-time it
was. The horses, dripping with sweat, and with patches
of foam under their harness, moved round and round
steadily to the cheery whistle of the driver.

The wild, imperious song of the bell-metal cog-wheel
had sung into Milton's ears till it had become a torture,
and every time he lifted his eyes to the beautiful far-off

sky, where the clouds floated like ships, a lump of rebellious anger rose in his throat. Why should he work in this choking dust and deafening noise while the hawks could sail and sweep from hill to hill with nothing to do but play?

Occasionally his uncle, the feeder, smiled down upon him, his face black as a negro, great goggles of glass and wire-cloth covering his merry eyes. His great good-nature shone out in the flash of his white teeth, behind his dusky beard, and he tried to encourage Milton with his smile. He seemed tireless to the other hands. He was so big and strong. He had always been Milton's boyish hero. So Milton crowded back the tears that came into his eyes, and would not let his uncle see how childish he was.

A spectator riding along the road would have remarked upon the lovely setting for this picturesque scene — the low swells of prairie, shrouded with faint, misty light from the unclouded sky, the flaming colors of the trees, the faint sound of cow-bells, and the cheery sound of the machine. But to be a tourist and to be a toiler in a scene like this are quite different things.

They were anxious to finish the setting by noon, and so the feeder was crowding the cylinder to its limit, rolling the grain in with slow and apparently effortless swaying from side to side, half buried in the loose yellow straw. But about eleven o'clock the machine came to a stand, to wait while a broken tooth was being replaced, and Milton fled from the terrible dust beside the measuring spout, and was shaking the chaff out of his clothing, when he heard a high, snappy, nasal voice call down from the straw-pile. A tall man, with a face completely masked in dust, was speaking to Mr. Jennings: —

"Say, young man, I guess you'll haf to send another man up here. It's poorty stiff work f'r two; yes, sir, poorty stiff."

"There, there! I thought you'd cry 'cavy,'" laughed Mr. Jennings. "I told you it wasn't the place for an old man."

"Old man," snarled the figure in the straw. "I ain't so old but I can daown you, sir, — yessir, condemmit, yessir!"

"I'm your man," replied Jennings, smiling up at him.

The man rolled down the side of the stack, disappearing in a cloud of dust and chaff. When he came to light, Milton saw a tall, gaunt old man of sixty years of age, or older. Nothing could be seen but a dusty expanse of face, ragged beard, and twinkling, sharp little eyes. His color was lost, his eyes half hid. Without waiting for ceremony, the men clenched. The crowd roared with laughter, for though Jennings was the younger, the older man was a giant still, and the struggle lasted for some time. He made a gallant fight, but his breath gave out, and he lay at last flat on his back.

"I wish I was your age, young man," he said ruefully, as he rose. "I'd knock the heads o' these young scamps t'gether, — yessir! — I could do it, too!"

"Talk's a good dog, uncle," said a young man.

The old man turned on him so ferociously that he fled.

"Run, condemn yeh! I own y' can beat me at that." His face was not unpleasant, though his teeth were mainly gone, and his skin the color of leather and wrinkled as a pan of cream. His eyes had a certain sparkle of fun that belied his rasping voice, which seemed to have the power to lift a boy clean off his feet. His frame was bent and thin, but of great height and breadth, bony and tough as hickory. At some far time vast muscles must have rolled on those giant limbs, but toil had bent and stiffened him.

"Never been sick a day 'n my life; no, sir!" he said, in his rapid, rasping, emphatic way, as they were riding across the stubble to dinner. "And, by gol! I c'n stand as long at the tail of a stacker as any man, sir. Dummed if I turn my hand for any man in the state; no, sir; no, sir! But if I do two men's works, I am goin' to have two men's pay — that's all, sir!"

Jennings laughed and said: "All right, uncle. I'll send another man up there this afternoon."

The old man seemed to take a morbid delight in the hard and dirty places, and his endurance was marvellous. He could stand all day at the tail of a stacker, tirelessly pushing the straw away with an indifferent air, as if it were all mere play.

He measured the grain the next day, because it promised to be a noisier and dustier job than working in the straw, and it was in this capacity that Milton came to know and to hate him, and to associate him with that most hated of all tasks, the holding of sacks. To a twelve-year-old boy it seems to be the worst job in the world.

All day, while the hawks wheel and dip in the glorious air, and the trees glow like banks of roses; all day, while the younger boys are tumbling about the sunlit straw, to be forced to stand holding sacks, like a convict, was maddening. Daddy, whose rugged features, bent shoulders, and ragged cap loomed through the suffocating, blinding dust, necessarily came to seem like the jailer who held the door to freedom.

And when the dust and noise and monotony seemed the very hardest to bear, the old man's cackling laugh was sure to rise above the howl of the cylinder.

"Nem mind, sonny! Chaff ain't pizen; dust won't hurt ye a mite." And when Milton was unable to laugh, the old man tweaked his ear with his leathery thumb and finger.

Then he shouted long, disconnected yarns, to which Milton could make neither head nor tail, and which grew at last to be inaudible to him, just as the steady boom and snarl of the great machine did. Then he fell to studying the old man's clothes, which were a wonder to him. He spent a good deal of time trying to discover which were the original sections of the coat, and especially of the vest, which was ragged and yellow with age, with the cotton batting working out; and yet Daddy took the greatest care of it, folding it carefully and putting it away during the heat of the day out of reach of the crickets.

One of his peculiarities, as Mrs. Jennings learned on the second day, was his habit of coming to breakfast. But he always earned all he got, and more too; and, as it was probable that his living at home was frugal, Mrs. Jennings smiled at his thrift, and quietly gave him his breakfast if he arrived late, which was not often.

He had bought a little farm not far away, and settled down into a mode of life which he never afterward changed. As he was leaving at the end of the third day, he said: —

"Now, sir, if you want any bootcherin' done, I'm y'r man. I don't turn m' hand over f'r any man in the state; no, sir! I c'n git a hawg on the gambrils jest a leetle quicker'n any other man I ever see; yes, sir; by gum!"

"All right, uncle; I'll send for you when I'm ready to kill."

II

HOG-KILLING was one of the events of a boy's life on a Western farm, and Daddy was destined to be associated in the minds of Shep and Milton with another disagreeable job, that of building the fire and carrying water.

It was very early on a keen, biting morning in November when Daddy came driving into the yard with his rude, long-runnered sled, one horse half his length behind the other in spite of the driver's clucking. He was delighted to catch the boys behind in the preparation.

" A-a-h-h-r-r-h-h ! " he rasped out, " you lazy vaga-
bon's ? Why ain't you got that fire blazin' ? WHAT
the devil do y' mean, you rascals ! Here it is broad
daylight, and that fire not built. I vum, sir, you need
a thrashin', the whole kit an bilun' of ye; yessir !
Come, come, come ! hustle now, stir your boots !
hustle y'r boots — ha ! ha ! ha ! "

It was of no use to plead cold weather and damp
chips.

" What has that got to do with it, sir ? I vum, sir,
when I was your age, I could make a fire of green
red-oak; yessir ! Don't talk to me of colds ! Stir
your stumps and get warm, sir ! "

The old man put up his horses (and fed them
generously with oats), and then went to the house to
ask for " a leetle something hot — mince pie or sassidge."
His request was very modest, but, as a matter of fact,
he sat down and ate a very hearty breakfast, while the
boys worked away at the fire under the big kettle.

The hired man, under Daddy's direction, drew the
bob-sleighs into position on the sunny side of the corn-
crib, and arranged the barrel at the proper slant, while
the old man ground his knives, Milton turning the
grindstone — another hateful task, which Daddy's
stories could not alleviate.

Daddy never finished a story. If he started in to
tell about a horse trade, it infallibly reminded him of
a cattle trade, and talking of cattle switched him off
upon logging, and logging reminded him of some
heavy snow-storm he had known. Each parenthesis

M

outgrew its proper limits, till he forgot what should
have been the main story.   His stories had some com-
pensation, for when he stopped to try to recollect where
he was, the pressure on the grindstone was released.

At last the water was hot, and the time came to seize
the hogs.   This was the old man's great moment.   He
stood in the pen and shrieked with laughter while the
hired men went rolling, one after the other, upon the
ground, or were bruised against the fence by the rush of
the burly swine.

"You're a fine lot," he laughed.   " Now, then, sir,
grab 'im !   Why don't ye nail 'im?   I vum, sir, if I
couldn't do better'n that, sir, I'd sell out; I would, sir,
by gol!   Get out o' the way!"

With a lofty scorn he waved aside all help and stalked
like a gladiator toward the pigs huddled in one corner of
the pen.   And when the selected victim was rushing by
him, his long arm and great bony hand swept out,
caught him by the ear, and flung him upon his side,
squealing with deafening shrillness.   But in spite of
his smiling concealment of effort, Daddy had to lean
against the fence and catch his breath even while he
boasted : —

"I'm an old codger, sir, but I'm worth — a dozen o'
you — spindle-legged chaps; dum me if I ain't, sir!"

His pride in his ability to catch and properly kill a
hog was as genuine as the old knight-errant's pride in
his ability to stick a knife into another steel-clothed
brigand like himself.   When the slain shote was swung
upon the planking on the sled before the barrel, Daddy

rested, while the boys filled the barrel with water from the kettle.

There was always a weird charm about this stage of the work to the boys. The sun shone warm and bright in the lee of the corn-crib; the steam rose up, white and voluminous, from the barrel; the eaves dropped steadily; the hens ventured near, nervously, but full of curiosity, while the men laughed and joked with Daddy, starting him off on long stories, and winking at each other when his back was turned.

At last he mounted his planking, selecting Mr. Jennings to pull upon the other handle of the hog-hook. He considered he conferred a distinct honor in this selection.

"The time's been, sir, when I wouldn't thank any man for his help. No, sir, wouldn't thank 'im."

"What do you do with these things?" asked one of the men, kicking two iron candlesticks which the old man laid conveniently near.

"Scrape a hawg with them, sir. What do y' s'pose, you numskull?"

"Well, I never saw anything —"

"You'll have a chance mighty quick, sir. Grab ahold, sir! Swing 'im around — there! Now easy, easy! Now then, one, two; one, two — that's right."

While he dipped the porker in the water, pulling with his companion rhythmically upon the hook, he talked incessantly, mixing up scraps of stories and boastings of what he could do, with commands of what he wanted the other man to do.

"The best man I ever worked with. *Now turn 'im,
turn 'im!*" he yelled, reaching over Jennings's wrist.
"Grab under my wrist. There! won't ye never learn
how to turn a hawg? *Now out with 'im!*" was his
next wild yell, as the steaming hog was jerked out of
the water upon the planking. "Now try the hair on
them ears! Beautiful scald," he said, clutching his hand
full of bristles and beaming with pride. "Never see
anything finer. Here, Bub, a pail of hot water, quick!
Try one of them candlesticks! They ain't no better
scraper than the bottom of an old iron candlestick; no,
sir! Dum your new-fangled scrapers! I made a bet
once with old Jake Ridgeway that I could scrape the
hair off'n two hawgs, by gum, quicker'n he could one.
Jake was blowin' about a new scraper he had. . . .

"Yes, yes, yes, dump it right into the barrel. Condemmit! Ain't you got no gumption? . . . So Sim
Smith, he held the watch. Sim was a mighty good hand
t' work with; he was about the only man I ever sawed
with who didn't ride the saw. He could jerk a cross-
cut saw. . . . Now let him in again, now, *he-ho*, once
again! *Rool him over now;* that foreleg needs a tech o'
water. Now out with him again; that's right, that's
right! By gol, a beautiful scald as ever I see!"

Milton, standing near, caught his eye again. "Clean
that ear, sir! What the devil you standin' there for?"
He returned to his story after a pause. "A — n — d
Jake, he scraped away — *hyare!*" he shouted suddenly,
"don't ruggle the skin like that! Can't you see the
way I do it? Leave it smooth as a baby, sir — yessir!"

He worked on in this way all day, talking unceasingly, never shirking a hard job, and scarcely showing fatigue at any moment.

"I'm short o' breath a leetle, that's all; never git tired, but my wind gives out. Dum cold got on me, too."

He ate a huge supper of liver and potatoes, still working away hard at an ancient horse trade, and when he drove off at night, he had not yet finished a single one of the dozen stories he had begun.

III

BUT pitching grain and hog-killing were on the lower levels of his art, for above all else Daddy loved to be called upon to play the fiddle for dances. He "officiated" for the first time at a dance given by one of the younger McTurgs. They were all fiddlers themselves, — had been for three generations, — but they seized the opportunity of helping Daddy and at the same time of relieving themselves of the trouble of furnishing the music while the rest danced.

Milton attended this dance, and saw Daddy for the first time earning his money pleasantly. From that time on the associations around his personality were less severe, and they came to like him better. He came early, with his old fiddle in a time-worn white-pine box. His hair was neatly combed to the top of his long, narrow head, and his face was very clean. The boys all greeted him with great pleasure, and asked him where he would sit.

" Right on that table, sir; put a chair up there."

He took his chair on the kitchen-table as if it were a throne.   He wore huge moccasins of moose-hide on his feet, and for special occasions like this added a paper collar to his red woollen shirt.   He took off his coat and laid it across his chair for a cushion.   It was all very funny to the young people, but they obeyed him laughingly, and while they " formed on," he sawed his violin and coaxed it up to concert pitch, and twanged it and banged it into proper tunefulness.

" A-a-a-ll ready there ! " he rasped out, with prodigious force.   " Everybody git into his place ! "   Then, lifting one huge foot, he put the fiddle under his chin, and, raising his bow till his knuckles touched the strings, he yelled, " Already, G'LANG ! " and brought his foot down with a startling bang on the first note.   *Rye doodle doo, doodle doo.*

As he went on and the dancers fell into rhythm, the clatter of heavy boots seemed to thrill him with old-time memories, and he kept boisterous time with his foot, while his high, rasping nasal rang high above the confusion of tongues and heels and swaying forms.

" *Ladies'* gran' change !   FOUR hands round !   *Balance all ! Elly*-man left !   Back to play-cis."

His eyes closed in a sort of intoxication of pleasure, but he saw all that went on in some miraculous way.

" *First* lady lead to the right — *toodle rum rum ! Gent* foller after (step along thar) !   Four hands round — "

The boys were immensely pleased with him.   They delighted in his antics rather than in his tunes, which were exceedingly few and simple. They seemed never to be able to get enough of one tune which he called " Honest John," and which he played in his own way, accompanied by a chant which he meant, without a doubt, to be musical.

" Hon-ers tew your pardners — *tee teedle deedle dee dee dee dee!* Stand up straight an' put on your style! *Right* an' left four — "

The hat was passed by the floor-manager during the evening, and Daddy got nearly three dollars, which delighted Milton very much.

At supper he insisted on his prerogative, which was to take the prettiest girl out to supper.

" Look-a-here, Daddy, ain't that crowdin' the mourners ? " objected the others.

" What do you mean by that, sir ? No, sir! Always done it, in Michigan and Yark State both ; yes, sir."

He put on his coat ceremoniously, while the tittering girls stood about the room waiting. He did not delay. His keen eyes had made selection long before, and, approaching Rose Watson with old-fashioned, elaborate gallantry, he said : " *May* I have the pleasure ? " and marched out triumphantly, amidst shouts of laughter.

His shrill laugh rang high above the rest at the table, as he said : " I'm the youngest man in this crowd, sir! Demmit, I bet a hat I c'n dance down any man in this crowd ; yes, sir. The old man can do it yet."

They all took sides in order to please him.

" I'll bet he can," said Hugh McTurg; " I'll bet a dollar on Daddy."

"I'll take the bet," said Joe Randall, and with great noise the match was arranged to come the first thing after supper.

"All right, sir; any time, sir.   I'll let you know the old man is on earth yet."

While the girls were putting away the supper dishes, the young man lured Daddy out into the yard for a wrestling-match, but some others objected.

"Oh, now, that won't do!   If Daddy was a young man — "

"What do you mean, sir?   I am young enough for you, sir.   Just let me get ahold o' you, sir, and I'll show you, you young rascal! you dem jackanapes!" he ended, almost shrieking with rage, as he shook his fist in the face of his grinning tormentors.

His friends held him back with much apparent alarm, and ordered the other fellows away.

"There, there, Daddy, I wouldn't mind him!   I wouldn't dirty my hands on him; he ain't worth it. Just come inside, and we'll have that dancing-match now."

Daddy reluctantly returned to the house, and, having surrendered his violin to Hugh McTurg, was ready for the contest.   As he stepped into the middle of the room he was not altogether ludicrous.   His rusty trousers were bagged at the knee, and his red woollen stockings showed between the tops of his moccasins and his pantaloon legs, and his coat, utterly characterless as to color and cut, added to the stoop in his shoulders; and yet there was a rude sort of grace and a certain dignity about his bearing which kept down laughter. They were to have a square dance of the old-fashioned sort.

" *Farrm* on," he cried, and the fiddler struck up the first note of the Virginia Reel. Daddy led out Rose, and the dance began. He straightened up till his tall form towered above the rest of the boys like a weather-beaten pine tree, as he balanced and swung and led and called off the changes with a voice full of imperious command.

The fiddler took a malicious delight toward the last in quickening the time of the good old dance, and that put the old man on his mettle.

" Go it, ye young rascal!" he yelled. He danced like a boy and yelled like a demon, catching a laggard here and there, and hurling them into place like tops, while he kicked and stamped, wound in and out and waved his hands in the air with a gesture which must have dated back to the days of Washington. At last, flushed, breathless, but triumphant, he danced a final breakdown to the tune of " Leather Breeches," to show he was unsubdued.

IV

But these rare days passed away. As the country grew older it lost the wholesome simplicity of pioneer days, and Daddy got a chance to play but seldom. He no longer pleased the boys and girls — his music was too monotonous and too simple. He felt this very deeply. Once in a while he broke forth in protest against the changes.

"The boys I used to trot on m' knee are gittin' too high-toned. They wouldn't be found dead with old Deering, and then the preachers are gittin' thick, and howlin' agin dancin', and the country's filling up with Dutchmen, so't I'm left out."

As a matter of fact, there were few homes now where Daddy could sit on the table, in his ragged vest and rusty pantaloons, and play "Honest John," while the boys thumped about the floor. There were few homes where the old man was even a welcome visitor, and he felt this rejection keenly. The women got tired of see-ing him about, because of his uncleanly habits of spitting, and his tiresome stories. Many of the old neighbors died or moved away, and the young people went West or to the cities. Men began to pity him rather than laugh at him, which hurt him more than their ridicule. They began to favor him at threshing or at the fall hog-killing.

" Oh, you're getting old, Daddy ; you'll have to give up this heavy work. Of course, if you feel able to do it, why, all right ! Like to have you do it, but I guess we'll have to have a man to do the heavy lifting, I s'pose."

" I s'pose not, sir ! I am jest as able to yank a hawg as ever, sir ; yes, sir, demmit — demmit ! Do you think I've got one foot in the grave ? "

Nevertheless, Daddy often failed to come to time on appointed days, and it was painful to hear him trying to explain, trying to make light of it all.

" M' caugh wouldn't let me sleep last night. A gol-dum leetle, nasty, ticklin' caugh, too; but it kept me awake, fact was, an' — well, m' wife, she said I hadn't better come. But don't you worry, sir; it won't happen again, sir; no, sir."

His hands got stiffer year by year, and his simple tunes became practically a series of squeaks and squalls. There came a time when the fiddle was laid away almost altogether, for his left hand got caught in the cog-wheels of the horse-power, and all four of the fingers on that hand were crushed. Thereafter he could only twang a little on the strings. It was not long after this that he struck his foot with the axe and lamed himself for life.

As he lay groaning in bed, Mr. Jennings went in to see him and tried to relieve the old man's feelings by telling him the number of times he had practically cut his feet off, and said he knew it was a terrible hard thing to put up with.

" Gol dummit, it ain't the pain," the old sufferer yelled, " it's the dum awkwardness. I've chopped all my life; I can let an axe in up to the maker's name, and hew to a hair-line; yes, sir! It was jest them dum new mittens my wife made; they was s' slippery," he ended with a groan.

As a matter of fact, the one accident hinged upon the other. It was the failure of his left hand, with its useless fingers, to do its duty, that brought the axe down upon his foot. The pain was not so much physical as mental. To think that he, who could hew to a hairline, right and left hand, should cut his own foot like a ten-year-old boy — that scared him. It brought age

and decay close to him.   For the first time in his life he
felt that he was fighting a losing battle.

A man like this lives so much in the flesh, that when
his limbs begin to fail him everything else seems slipping
away.   He had gloried in his strength.   He had exulted
in the thrill of his life-blood and in the swell of his vast
muscles; he had clung to the idea that he was strong as
ever, till this last blow came upon him, and then he
began to think and to tremble.

When he was able to crawl about again, he was a
different man.   He was gloomy and morose, snapping
and snarling at all that came near him, like a wounded
bear.   He was alone a great deal of the time during the
winter following his hurt.   Neighbors seldom went in,
and for weeks he saw no one but his hired hand, and
the faithful, dumb little old woman, his wife, who moved
about without any apparent concern or sympathy for his
suffering.   The hired hand, whenever he called upon
the neighbors, or whenever questions were asked, said
that Daddy hung around over the stove most of the
time, paying no attention to any one or anything.   " He
ain't dangerous 't all," he said, meaning that Daddy was
not dangerously ill.

Milton rode out from school one winter day with
Bill, the hand, and was so much impressed with his
story of Daddy's condition that he rode home with him.
He found the old man sitting bent above the stove,
wrapped in a quilt, shivering and muttering to himself.
He hardly looked up when Milton spoke to him, and
seemed scarcely to comprehend what he said.

Milton was much alarmed at the terrible change, for the last time he had seen him he had towered above him, laughingly threatening to "warm his jacket," and now here he sat, a great hulk of flesh, his mind flickering and flaring under every wind of suggestion, soon to go out altogether.

In reply to questions he only muttered with a trace of his old spirit: "I'm all right. Jest as good a man as I ever was, only I'm cold. I'll be all right when spring comes, so 't I c'n git outdoors. Somethin' to warm me up, yessir; I'm cold, that's all."

The young fellow sat in awe before him, but the old wife and Bill moved about the room, taking very little interest in what the old man said or did. Bill at last took down the violin. "I'll wake him up," he said. "This always fetches the old feller. Now watch 'im."

"Oh, don't do that!" Milton said in horror. But Bill drew the bow across the strings with the same stroke that Daddy always used when tuning up.

He lifted his head as Bill dashed into "Honest John," in spite of Milton's protest. He trotted his feet after a little and drummed with his hands on the arms of his chair, then smiled a little in a pitiful way. Finally he reached out his right hand for the violin and took it into his lap. He tried to hold the neck with his poor, old, mutilated left hand, and burst into tears.

"Don't you do that again, Bill," Milton said. "It's better for him to forget that. Now you take the best care of him you can to-night. I don't think he's going to live long; I think you ought to go for the doctor right off."

"Oh, he's been like this for the last two weeks; he ain't sick, he's jest old, that's all," replied Bill, brutally.

And the old lady, moving about without passion and without speech, seemed to confirm this; and yet Milton was unable to get the picture of the old man out of his mind. He went home with a great lump in his throat.

The next morning, while they were at breakfast, Bill burst wildly into the room.

"Come over there, all of you; we want you."

They all looked up much scared. "What's the matter, Bill?"

"Daddy's killed himself," said Bill, and turned to rush back, followed by Mr. Jennings and Milton.

While on the way across the field Bill told how it all happened.

"He wouldn't go to bed, the old lady couldn't make him, and when I got up this morning I didn't think nothin' about it. I s'posed, of course, he'd gone to bed all right; but when I was going out to the barn I stumbled across something in the snow, and I felt around, and there he was. He got hold of my revolver someway. It was on the shelf by the washstand, and I s'pose he went out there so 't we wouldn't hear him. I dassn't touch him," he said, with a shiver; "and the old woman, she jest slumped down in a chair an' set there — wouldn't do a thing — so I come over to see you."

Milton's heart swelled with remorse. He felt guilty because he had not gone directly for the doctor. To think that the old sufferer had killed himself was horrible and seemed impossible.

The wind was blowing the snow, cold and dry, across the yard, but the sun shone brilliantly upon the figure in the snow as they came up to it. There Daddy lay. The snow was in his scant hair and in the hollow of his wide, half-naked chest. A pistol was in his hand, but there was no mark upon him, and Milton's heart leaped with quick relief. It was delirium, not suicide.

There was a sort of majesty in the figure half buried in the snow. His hands were clenched, and there was a frown of resolution on his face, as if he had fancied Death coming, and had gone defiantly forth to meet him.

HORSUS CHAWIN' HAY

I TELL yeh whut! The chankin'
   Which the tired horses makes
When you've slipped the harness off'm,
   An' shoved the hay in flakes
From the hay-mow overhead,
   Is jest about the equal of any pi-anay;
They's nothin' soun's s' cumftabul
   As horsus chawin' hay.

I love t' hear 'em chankin',
   Jest a-grindin' slow and low,
With their snoots a-rootin' clover
   Deep as their ol' heads 'll go,
It's kind o' sort o' restin'
   To a feller's bones, I say,
It soun's s' mighty cumftabul —
   The horsus chawin' hay.

Gra-onk, gra-onk, gra-onk!
   In a stiddy kind o' tone,
Not a tail a-waggin' to 'um,
   N'r another sound 'r groan —
Fer the flies is gone a-snoozin'.
   Then I loaf around an' watch 'em
In a sleepy kind o' way,
   F'r they soun' so mighty cumftabul,
   As they rewt and chaw their hay.

An' it sets me thinkin' sober
  Of the days of '53,
When we pioneered the prairies —
  M' wife an' dad an' me,
In a dummed ol' prairie-schooner,
  In a rough-an'-tumble way,
Sleepin' out at nights, to music
  Of the horsus chawin' hay.

Or I'm thinkin' of my comrades
  In the fall of '63,
When I rode with ol' Kilpatrick
  Through an' through ol' Tennessee.
I'm a-layin' in m' blanket
  With my head agin a stone,
Gazin' upwards toward the North Star —
  Billy Sykes and Davy Sloan
  A-snorin' in a buck-saw kind o' way,
An' me a-layin', listenin'
  To the horsus chawin' hay.

It strikes me turrible cur'ous
  That a little noise like that,
Can float a feller backward
  Like the droppin' of a hat;
An' start his throat a-achin',
  Make his eyes wink that a-way —
They ain't no sound that gits me,
  Like horsus chawin' hay.

N

BLACK EPHRAM

This good should be for every man
  That walks the earth beneath the sky,
Free should he be to build and plan,
  And in contentment die.

BLACK EPHRAM

WHEN Wesley Rogers returned from the South he brought back with him a black man. It took but a few days for the whole country to know of it, and to find out that he had been a slave and that his name was Uncle Eph. The boys followed him as he walked up the street of Rock River, and stood to watch him as he clambered into the wagon of one of Wesley's neighbors, who was in town with a load of corn.

Uncle Eph was perfectly black and had a mighty chest, though his legs were considerably less powerful. His head was well shaped, his face was grave, and his eyes unusually keen for a negro. He could read a little, Wesley said, and he was very religious. Though very far from being a white man painted black, he was a rather superior negro.

Wesley was a churchman himself, and had been attracted to Eph by his power as an exhorter and as a singer. Wesley had the gift himself, and sang tenor to Uncle Eph's bass with great delight as they rode home through the warm September evening.

It was all strange to the negro. He had readily consented to come North because to him it was a mystical " God's country." He went as a friend, not as a servant, for Wesley had no touch of authority in him. His hired men were always as much boss as himself.

The big black man was dazzled by his reception in the county. Everybody seemingly took a friend's interest in him, and as he was the only negro in the country at that time, the men shook hands with him or shouted at him with the same peculiar inflection they used when addressing each other. He could not accustom himself to this at once. It was all so strange.

He worked for Wesley during the first year that he lived in the country, and he sat at the table with the rest after some timid protest.

"I do' know, Misto Wesley, if wheddo I should do dat."

"Certainly; sit down," Wesley said. "You ain't a slave any more. You're my hired man. Sit down."

"Well, you see, Missis she might —"

"Good land, no; sit down, Eph. Have sense," Mrs. Rogers said vigorously.

And thereafter he humbly took his seat by the children.

It was long before the wonder of it wore off, but at last he came to feel at ease. He seemed at last to feel his right to come and go as others did.

Mrs. Rogers explained to Mrs. Adams: "So long as he is as clean as we are, I don't see as I've any call to object, and he certainly is neat."

The children liked him very much, and on evenings in the kitchen he often took the entire group of yellow-headed youngsters in his great arms, and, with his mighty voice subdued to a soft croon, sang the baby to sleep.

It was a moving sight, — the great black surrounded by his mob of pale children.

Mrs. Rogers used to sit and listen to him in silence, until the striking clock roused her with a start and a sigh.

"Well, Eph, you do make time fly! Children, rouse up, now. Gimme the baby, Eph. You're a great hand with babies, I must say. She's been a-worritin' all day to-day, but — "

Sometimes he sang songs they could not understand. Strange, wild chants, in a half-voice that made the shivers run over Mrs. Rogers. She used to speak up irritably : —

"Eph, what in the world you singing now?"

"I can't tell you quite, Missis. It's about de land ob de lion. Darky wants to go back. White man let me go. I want 'o go back, — back to de land ob de lion!" Evidently something sweet and far-off rose within him as he sang these songs.

He became a great feature in the protracted meetings in the neighborhood. People came long roads to hear him sing. Wesley's enthusiasm was justified when Eph rose one night and sang, "Form a Line, Elder," during his first winter in the North.

After that the meeting prospered, and "Bro. Ephram" was recognized as a valuable exhorter. Also Bro. Rogers had many callers of an evening, and then Eph "patted juber," and sang "Jordan Am a Hard Road to Trabbel," "Sinner, Let Me Go," "Old Mule," and many other songs of the plantation.

He grew in respect for himself, but he did not lose his balance. He was naturally a well-poised character. He soon perceived that to retain any servility, or to doubt the genuineness of the good will expressed, would be making his neighbors awkward and angry. He accepted their courtesy without comment.

He ceased calling people by their first names in the Southern way. He called them Missis Jones and Misto Bacon. He had little dialect, and lost very soon a large number of his most peculiar phrases. His thickness of utterance remained, and in moments of excitement, his African tongue came back, together with a wild chant that delighted the people very much. There were times when he seemed sad, — perhaps he was thinking of the peach trees and sunlight of Georgia.

Life did not go altogether smoothly for him, however. There were a few shiftless woodsmen living around the mill who were outraged that a negro should be treated like a white man. They muttered threats about shooting, but Bacon and Councill told Eph he need not fear them. He tried not to be disturbed by their snarling, but he could not shake off all sense of his terrible disability before the law.

He was troubled most by an old " copperhead " who owned a farm a little way up the river. Old man Beckett was reported to have come into Cedar County from Ohio, where his presence was not valued. He was a tall, grim, red-haired man of fifty, with immense shoulders, which he always carried edgewise to the front like a fighting bull. His right eye was "crooked," and his voice was harsh and rasping.

He was known to be a coward and braggart, but a braggart with great discretion. He was loud in his threats against Uncle Eph at once. "I ain't goin' to have no damn nigger a-swellin' around over me," he said one night in the presence of Councill and several others at the March school meeting.

Councill mildly interposed a word: "He don't seem to be swellin' around, so far as I can see, he is tendin' to his own knittin' full as well as some other folks I know."

Beckett stormed on. "Well, he's no business to come up here tryin' to get on an equality with white folks."

"He won't have to try very hard to get on a level with some folks," said Wesley with a smile.

"I don't know about that," put in Adams. "He'd get pretty low if he did."

Beckett turned from one to the other, livid with rage.

"Yes, you'd all take up with a damn nigger — y'r all damned Abolitionists."

"Tut! tut! friend Beckett," said Jennings; "the war is over, the whole matter is settled, and we — "

"Well, it ain't settled so far as I am concerned. I'll be God damned if any nigger — "

Bacon interrupted his hoarse howl by clutching his shoulder.

"If you're so brisk for war I think you can be accommodated. Now shut up, or I'm damned if I don't heave yeh through the window. I've heerd about all your yap I kin stand!"

Beckett looked down at the floor and muttered under his breath. Bacon went on, with savage intensity : —

"I was born south of Mason and Dixon's line m'self. I ain't got no p'ticler love for niggers, but as long as they go about peaceably and don't trouble me I ain't got no say about what they shan't do. As for equality — I'd a damn sight rather have old Eph in my house than you. Now, don't let me hear any more o' your yap !"

This was about the longest speech Bacon ever made, and it silenced Beckett so far as any public utterance was concerned, but thereafter he never met Eph on the road or passed him working the fields without cursing him and lashing at him with his whip.

Notwithstanding the kindness of the people, Eph felt that he would rather live alone, so in his second year rented a little farm down on the river bottom, and fitted up the old log hut there, so that he could keep house by himself. The people assisted him a little in ploughing and in cutting his grain, and he got along nicely. The next year he bought a bony old horse and a noisy democrat wagon, and felt very proud of it.

Beckett was the only disturbing factor in his life. He never failed to stop and revile him as he drove along on his way to Rock River, but Uncle Eph never complained. He bore it all in silence.

Bacon and Councill returning from town one day, came upon Beckett yelling ferocious threats at Uncle Eph, who was working quietly in his garden, not hearing, apparently, the infuriate howling of his enemy.

When they came near, Beckett drove hastily away. Councill pulled up, and Uncle Eph came to the fence, smiling. It was lonesome down there on the flat, and he liked to have folks stop and chat.

"Good evenin', Mist' Councill.

"Good evenin', Mist' Bacon; fine evenin'."

"Say, Eph, why don't you go out and whale the daylights out o' that old skunk?" said Councill.

Uncle Eph looked troubled. "Well, sah, I is tempted, sho'ly. I ask de Lawd to help me, sah; elsewise I would, sho'."

"It would be a religious duty," Councill said. "The next time he comes by just give him a wheltin' that he'll remember."

Uncle Eph changed his feet a time or two. "Well, Mist' Councill, I feels mighty like it, I do assu' you; but I don't just 'xactly know what folks gwine say."

"Oh, that's it, is it?"

"Yessah. You see, down South —"

Bacon interrupted: "You ain't down South; you're up North. If you'll thrash the pizen out o' that old whelp, I'll see that you ain't troubled by anybody else afterward."

"I'll stand by you, too," Councill said. Eph's face shone with a sort of joyful relief. "Well, sah, you can 'pend on me, sah. He won't call old Eph any mo' bad names. De Lawd willun, I'se 'bleeged to trounce him de very nex' time he come along an' holleh."

The men laughed and drove on. "I'd like to see the fun," said Councill.

Not long after that Beckett, being in a bad mood, pulled up again before Eph's gate and yelled for him to come out and take his medicine.

Eph was in the barn and thought to keep out of sight, but at last he grew impatient of the man's voice and came to the door.

"You go 'long. Don' stand there hollerin'."

Beckett grew more ferocious. "I'd get out and cut you into strips for a cent," he swore, menacing Eph with the whip.

"If I come out tha, sah, I trounce you sho'," Eph replied.

Beckett shook his whip at him. "You will? If you dare lay hands on me — "

Eph kept approaching. "You sho'ly do try me," he said.

Beckett's voice changed. "If you come within reach, I'll cut your heart out, you black dog. What business you got? Don't you come nearer — "

Uncle Eph still approached. "I ent 'fraid of yo' whip," he said with a calm inflection. He was almost within reach. He came slowly, with a look of battle in his eyes. His bare neck and arms glistened like old bronze worn with handling. There was something terrifying in his steady approach, unhurried, but relentless. His mind was made up.

Beckett lashed out at him with his whip. His worn old team, accustomed to his loud voice, did not lift their heads. Eph leaped suddenly within range.

The whip came down once, and only once, on the

black man's head. A sweeping clutch of his bear-like paw and Beckett came out over the wheel fighting like a wildcat, and the two men went to the ground rolling over and over in battle.

Now the negro's voice arose, the battle-gust came into his throat, and the murder-thirst into his heart. It seemed as if he could crush this man between the palms of his two hands.

"Aooah! yo' neber hit me again, yo' old Satan — yo' old debbil."

His words were lost in the deep roll of his growl. The dust arose from where they lay rolling and striking. The team had moved off down the road a little. Blows, curses, hoarse breathing, came out of the dust cloud.

At length Uncle Eph arose, and as he stood looking down at his quiescent adversary the dust of battle moved away slowly on the gentle wind. The white man did not rise at once. He was stunned and bloody and subdued. He got up at last and turned about in a daze, looking for his team. As he picked up his hat and whip, he looked at Eph sullenly, menacingly, but did not care to try again. As he walked away he looked so bedraggled and slouching and dusty that Eph's anger turned to amusement. His teeth shone first, and then his voice gurgled out in thick laughter.

"Yo' suttenly look like a secon' best rooster," he said.

Beckett turned. "I'll have the law on you," he said. "I'll put you where the dogs won't bite yeh."

Eph sobered. The law held strange terrors for him. The whip, a fist, he understood, but the law was an unknown, invisible, incomprehensible force. He stood in silence till Beckett climbed into his wagon and drove away.

The law! That meant a white man's power. That meant a rule which forever went against the black man. He had known many individual white people who were good and fine. He loved his old masters. They had both been kind and just; but his understanding of law was warped and incomplete. It was an intangible enginery which the white man in some way controlled for his own interest. It represented in some way the difference between the black and the white.

Personally he felt no fear of any living man, but this strange and awful power of the law terrorized him, and he went about all day very sober.

A general laugh went round the country when the battle became known. Practically everybody said: "Served the old skeesix right."

This gave little comfort to Eph, however, when the Sheriff rode into the yard a couple of days later with a warrant for him. He bowed his head in instant resignation, and his face was pitiful to see. "Misto Shirf, I jest want feed my chickens an' shut up de house."

"Why, of course," said the Sheriff, as he lounged in the buggy seat.

To Eph it was like going away forever. He looked

at his crops, his chickens, and his horse. He put down a big pan of water for the chickens and locked the door of his house and led his pony out.

"I jest like to take Ole Ben over to Misto Bacon's, sah, if you don't mind."

"Not at all. Just lead him behind. You'll be bailed out and be back to-night or to-morrow. So don't worry."

Bacon was hitched up ready to go to mill.

"Hello, Eph! Where you goun' with that Sheriff?"

Eph smiled rather pitifully. "I don't know, Misto Bacon. I jest gwine 'long o' him."

"What's up, Sam?" Bacon said, coming to the wagon wheel.

"Old Beckett has sworn out a warrant against Eph for 'sault and battery."

"The old whelp. You ain't mean enough to serve that warrant on an old nigger?"

"Had to do it, Bill. I can't pass on the justice of a warrant."

"Who issued it?"

"Brown."

"Well, I'll go right down to see Brown about it. It's a mean, sneaking trick. I told Eph I'd stand by him if he whaled Beckett, and I'll do it if it takes half my farm."

"He'll need a bondsman, sure; or he's jugged, you know."

"Well, I'll see about that."

Eph was deeply relieved to have Bacon go along

with him. Bacon made him tell the whole story, at
which they all roared. Eph's account of it seemed
very funny, though he did not intend it to be so.

" 'N' ye wallered him good, did ye ? "

" I sho'ly did trounce him to my best capacities,
sah," Eph said, in answer.

In some way he managed to put before Judge Brown
his fear of the law ; perhaps it was in his gesture, as
he bared his head in awe ; perhaps in the nervous
fumbling of his hands ; certainly in some way he
uttered the fear and awe of a human soul to whom
law has always meant injustice, bondage, and appro-
priation.

The bluff old lawyer heard Bacon through, and then
said, in his judicial tones : —

" I'm a Democrat. I believed in buying out the
slaves, but I propose to see justice done. The law
with me will not draw the color line. So far as possible I have always made law an instrument of justice
and liberty. You go home and attend to your affairs.
If Beckett does not withdraw his charge, you must
appear in November and stand trial, but I don't think
it will be serious. We'll see that the law is dealt out
with impartial hand. Your color will not count."

Bacon winked at the Judge, and said : " I think we
can induce Beckett to call it a fair fout and no favor."

The Judge remained non-committal. " I don't
know anything about that, but if a man comes in here
all battered up and swears out a warrant, I must issue
it."

Eph caught the tone if not all the words of the Judge's speech, and something vast and splendid came into his thought; for the first time in his life he caught a glimpse of freedom under law. His heart swelled till he ached with a wish to sob. His eyes filled with tears. He bowed his great woolly head over the Judge's hand with the gesture of a slave.

"Don't do that," said the Judge, sharply. "I'm not doing this for you because you're black, but because it's the law."

On the way home he sat silent beside Bacon, except now and then when he broke into a little joyful crooning phrase or uttered some religious ejaculation.

That night some neighbors passing by heard him praying in his cabin. His voice rose in fervent chant as he prayed God to bless the Judge and Bacon and all the good white folks who had been so kind to him.

And as the listeners — unimaginative farmer folk — rode on, they felt a queer lump rising in their throats. There was something moving in the voice of the old black man chanting praises of them to God, as he knelt there in his lonely cabin on the river sands.

o

ACROSS THE PICKET-LINE

AFTER we'd been a-chasin' old Hood
　　And penned him into Atlanty,
Uncle Billy, doggone him, stood
　　Around behind us t' make us anty;
A-diggin' dirt and a-cuttin' ditches,
　　F'r days and days, an' top o' that,
We slep', side-arms in our britches,
　　Ready t' fight at the drop o' the hat.

Wal! The rebel pickets got closer 'n' closer
　　Till blame near we could almost see
The kind o' fellers the Johnnies was,
　　An' talk as easy as you an' me
Out in the field here ploughin' corn,
　　An' gassin' across the dividin' line.
Yessir! An' there we'd set an' trade off lies
　　About the war, and provisions, tell,
Some feller 'd sing out, "Hunt y'r holes!
　　Give the last man sinjen' hell!"

Wal! Every night we c'd hear 'em sing
　　"Old Hundred," or "Salvation's Free,"
An' we'd join in and make things ring,
　　An' so we got t' know, y' see,
Jest when the Johnnies meant t' shell
　　'R charge next day, 'r spring a mine;
For when they'd plan'd t' give us hell
　　They'd sing of heaven all 'long the line.

Fact ! Yessir, sure's y'r born,
  I never see the singin' fail,
Always brought a storm next day,
  With bullets flyin' thick as hail,
An' them there Rebs a-scramblin' right
  Straight up to our blessed eyes —
Teeth gritted, faces white —
  An' yellin' fit to raise the skies.

'Fraid ? Not by a darn sight ! They
  Didn't know what *that* word meant.
No sir — they'd jest nacherly pray,
  An' wherever a man 'ud go, they went ;
They wa'n't no discount on their grit,
  And I don't bear 'em any spite.
We met like men, 'an settled it,
  And I guess they think it's settled right.

THE WAPSEYPINNICON TIGER

THE WAPSEYPINNICON TIGER

IT was Saturday night in Rock River. Teams covered with the dust of the August roads stood in rows along the sidewalks. Harvesting was in full drive, and the town was filled with nomads from the South, men who had worked their way North following the isothermal line of ripening wheat.

The farmers had driven in for provisions, their hands had come with them for an evening's outing. The streets swarmed with rough, lawless characters. Few women ventured abroad, but bands of yelling boys, feeling the unstable equilibrium of the atmosphere, fought or played, up and down before the saloons which were crowded to the doors.

The better class of settlers hitched up and drove away before nine o'clock, gathering together as many of their hands as possible, but others remained to see the fun, which every one felt to be coming.

It was reported that the "Wapsey gang" was in town. The Swedes from Rock Run were also well represented down at Ole's "Hole in the Wall." The Vesey boys and Steve Nagle had been seen, and last and most important, Bill Moriarity, "the Wapsey Tiger," was down at the red saloon.

Bill was brother to the deputy sheriff, who had been in his day the most feared of all the Wapsey gang. He it was who used to terrorize the constable, and make men like Steve Nagle quail when, on his infrequent sprees, he took offence at the sound of their voices. He dominated the gang, and ruled as if with naked sword in hand.

By the advice of Dr. Carver, Jim had been made constable of the town. The Doctor had quoted with great effect the experience of Boston in making the famous crook, Tukey, marshal, in the days when thugs ran the city in their own way. From being constable, Jim came naturally to be the deputy sheriff of the county and had given up drink entirely.

Bill, also from the Wapsey prairie, was quiet enough ordinarily, but when in liquor was ferocious as a panther. At such times no one dared to oppose him nor lay hands upon him, that is, no one but his brother, the deputy. Every law-abiding citizen regretted the infrequent visits of the Wapsey Tiger.

Constable Ranney, a tall, mild-mannered man, grew more and more nervous as the night drew on and reports came in about Bill. He kept sedulously out of sight after eight o'clock; in fact, he went to the mayor's office for comfort and reënforcement. He made a feeble effort to cover his flight by saying to several of the uneasy citizens on the street : —

" If I'm wanted, I'll be at the mayor's office. I'm going up to consult him."

This deceived no one. Every man and boy in Rock River knew that Ranney was afraid of Steve Nagle, to say nothing of Bill. They shouted calls at him as he went along the street, but they could not blame him very much. There was a sort of horse sense in keeping out of the Tiger's way.

The matter was being discussed in the mayor's office. Ridings was there, and Judge Brown, and two or three others. Foster, of the *Saturday Morning Call*, took a humorous view of the matter, the others did not. Foster quoted a line or two while sharpening a pencil : —

" Now, ' whether Roderigo kill Cassio, or Cassio Roderigo, all makes my gain ; ' I'm getting news."

" We may pull through all right yet," said the Mayor, a small man of a scholarly turn of mind, not fitted to cope with such crises.

" Depends on how soon Bill gets whiskey enough to put 'im to sleep," said Ridings, one of the councilmen.

A wild volley of whoops arose on the street. Ranney turned pale, the Mayor started up in his chair, Ridings set his lips grimly.

" The fun begins," said Foster. " Ranney, why ain't you out there on the street ? You'll miss something."

Ranney gave up all pretence. " I can hear just as well a little further off."

Judge Brown cleared his mouth of tobacco.

" Mr. Constable, we who are peaceable and not of powerful physical organization hire you to fight our battles for us. Mr. Mayor, order the constable to the scene of carnage."

The Mayor smiled faintly. " Mr. Constable, you know your duty."

" All too well," said Foster.

Another series of whoops arose mingled with maniacal laughter, and then a single wild voice in a sort of chant.

They all rushed to the window and looked out. Up the street, clearly outlined in the brilliant light of the moon, came the Tiger. He walked with a curious action as if his legs were made of steel springs. His bare feet glistened, his head was flung back in a wild gesture. He was Red Brian defying the English battle-line on Balley Moor.

" Come out, ye sons o' dogs, all o' ye, ye white-livered whelps. Come to me arrums, come, smell o' me fist." He leaped in the air. " Come down out o' that," he snarled, as he caught sight of the men in the mayor's office.

The heads disappeared, and the crowd on the street laughed, but the Tiger kept on waving his fist. " I can whip the worruld."

" Constable, arrest that man," commanded the Mayor.

" I can't do it, y'r honor," said Ranney, in deep distress.

Ridings broke out : " Things have come to a narrow lane, if we can't control the streets of our own town. If our constable can't or won't do his duty — "

Ranney, nearly sobbing in his shame and fear, dragged the star off his coat, and extended it to the Mayor.

" Take back the office, I don't want it. I didn't go into this thing to arrest grizzly bears nor crazy maniacs, for three dollars a day.   It's all very well for you fellows to sit here and order me to go and arrest that infernal devil; go do it yourself."

He flung the star on the floor, and walked toward the back stairway, " I'm going home."

Foster dryly remarked : " There's a certain degree of justice in what Mr. Ranney says.   There are too many commanding officers here and too few active warriors. There's just one man in this country who can arrest Bill Moriarity."

" You mean Jim ? "

" Yes, of course."

" Jim's in Cedarville."

" Then telegraph him."

" I telegraphed him an hour ago," said the Judge. " I knew we were in for trouble.   He ought to be here soon if he started promptly."

The Mayor sighed with relief.   " Well there's nothing to do but wait."

They looked out of the window at every fresh burst of noise.   The Tiger still paraded up and down, leaping into the air occasionally with a shrill " Wherroo ! " He had the weight of a lion and the activity of a leopard.   He was transformed from a slouchy, quietly humorous farmer into a demon.   Everybody gave way before him, and behind him a howling mob of admiring friends trailed.   Silence came only when he led the way into some saloon.

The better citizens kept dropping in at the mayor's office to ask why that man was not arrested.   The

Mayor cooled each one off by saying, "I'll deputize you to arrest him, if you wish."

While they sat waiting they heard the sound of hurry out in the street, then a word of command that brought them to a halt.

"Here comes Jim!"

Quick, powerful steps were heard on the stairway, and Jim came in. He was of moderate height, but the girth of his chest was enormous. His face was dark and handsome. His eyes had something placid and sorrowful in them. His drooping mustache half concealed a shapely mouth. Altogether he was a fine Irish type.

"Where is he?" he asked.

"In the red saloon, just now."

"Is he wild, b'ys?" Jim asked, in a hesitating way.

They felt no inclination to laugh.

"He is plumb crazy."

Jim gave a groan of sorrow and dismay.

"Murtherin' divils! What a task I have." He took out his big clasp-knife and laid it down.

"There's a gang with him too," said Ridings.

"I don't moind that, it's Billy, poor divil." He laid aside his revolver and took off his coat.

"It'll be desprit, b'ys," he said, with a sad quiver in his voice. "I can't shoot him, yer anner. It's me duty to arrest him, an' I will, but it's loike embracin' a lion to take Billy when he's dhrunk. He'll kill me if he can, if he's crazy, but I can't stroike him with a weapon, yer anner."

He looked sad and weak as he went out the door, but they knew the stuff of which his heart was made.

"If he isn't too dhrunk he'll come along when I lay me hand on his shouldher; if he's fightin' dhrunk, it's him or me," he said half to himself, as he went down the street, accompanied by Foster.

"Wan comfort," he added, in the same musing way, "Billy nivir shoots. It's fists wid him."

They heard a wild shouting up the street, where the open door of a saloon emptied its light upon the dark.

A crowd of men alternately surged in and out of the door, as if they moved away from a chained wildcat making plunges to the length of his chain. As they drew near, the howl of the drunken man could be heard as he raged against the barkeeper, who stood in deadly terror behind his bar pleading with him. He tried to assume a careless voice.

"Here, take all ye want. That's all right, have another drink — it's on me. That's all right — " Bill stopped suddenly like a hound scenting game.

"Here's Jim!" was the cry. "Get out o' the way, here's Jim."

Jim came through the crowd, his big, brown eyes fixed on Bill's wild face. The sadness in his face as well as its resolution awed the crowd.

"Billy, my boy, come home," he said gently. "Come home, Billy," and he laid his hand on his brother's shoulder.

There was no sign of relenting in Bill's eyes. He looked astonished, then his eyes contracted to red slits, his mouth squared at the corners, and his teeth showed in a horrible grin. His hand spread on the counter like a paw.

"To hell wid ye!" he answered.

"Get out o' me way," said Jim, without looking around. The crowd fell back, leaving a clear space.

"Come, Billy," he said again, but in a different tone. He saw a madman before him. With a quick, clutching, downward jerk, he rolled the Tiger to the floor and fell upon him. But the insane man rose under him with a bear-like action, and forced him to the floor on equal terms.

The two brothers were well matched in strength, but Jim, fighting because it was his duty, was hindered by his great love and admiration for his brother, who fought to kill. Jim broke loose and rose.

Bill sprang at him like a cat — Jim's left fist met him and rolled him on the floor.

"God forgive me!" Jim said, "I nivir struck me brother before."

He waited for the fallen man to rise. Bill seemed to bound from the ground. Again Jim knocked him rolling, and again he rose. This time he rose with a knife in his hand.

"Ah!" breathed the crowd.

"Shoot him!" said the barkeeper.

"Keep off!" said Jim. A new look came into his eyes. He was fighting for his life now. Again he met the infuriate with his fist, but the man fell at his feet, throwing him sprawling. Jim whirled upon his back, catching Bill's hand in a terrible grip. The blood was running from a gash in his cheek.

Over and over the two men rolled in the blood and sawdust. Notwithstanding their great bulk, they writhed with the bewildering convolutions of cats. Now Jim came to the top, now Bill, but always that right hand gripped the murderous wrist of the hand that held the knife. Jim fought silently, grimly. The brother uttered short, snarling imprecations, like a carnivorous animal at meat. He snapped at his brother with open jaws.

Again and again some volunteer raised a chair to strike Bill, but Jim said, " Lave be." His pride was touched. He would conquer him alone and he would not allow another man to strike his brother.

For ten minutes this struggle continued, and then Jim rose and sat astride the Tiger, who lay breathing heavily, cursing, raving, under his breath.

" Handcuff him ! " cried the crowd.

Jim shook his head. "There is no need," he said.

At the word " handcuff," the struggle began again. Bill wrenched loose suddenly and struck Jim again with the knife. The blow fell upon his collar-bone, and the blood poured forth again. Jim caught the deadly arm again in his left hand, and, lifting his terrible right hand, struck a blow upon the side of his brother's head, which laid him out limp and still.

" Out o' me way, b'ys," he said, as he rose holding the limp body in his hands. They made way for him, and he passed out into the street.

A shudder seized on the crowd. Jim was covered with sawdust and filth from the floor. His face was unrecognizable by reason of the terrible blows with fist and knife which had fallen there, and his shirt was dripping with blood also. He walked into the middle of the road with the stunned man held in his hands. The crowd made way for him as if he were a king. He put Bill down and knelt watchfully beside him.

"Call the Mayor," he said, "I'll have a word with him."

A moment later and the Mayor came hurrying down.

"What is it, Jim?"

He lifted a wild, sad face to the Mayor.

"Y'r anner, I ask permission to take Billy home. God knows it would kill him to wake in the jail, y'r anner. The b'y dawn't know what he's doin' at all. He'll be near dead with shame, when he sees the mark he's put on me. If he wakes in jail, 'twill break the heart of 'im. Y'r anner, you know Billy, when the whiskey's not in him, he's as fine a man as iver breathed the breath of life. May I take him home, y'r anner?"

The Mayor, deeply moved, nodded his head.

"Do what you think best, Jim."

"God bless ye, y'r anner. Will somebody find Billy's team?"

The team was brought, and the maniac was lifted into the wagon like a log.

Jim climbed in. "Give me the lines," he said to the man in the seat.

" Shan't I go with ye, Jim ? "

" Give me, I say."

The man surrendered the lines and leaped out of the wagon.

" Good night, y'r anner.   Good night, boys."

The wagon moved off in the glorious moonlight, with Jim sitting beside the drink-crazed man who lay on the bed of the wagon unbound, save by the grip of his brother's relentless right hand.

P

GOIN' BACK T'MORRER

(In the City)

I TELL ye, Sue, it ain't no use,
    I *can't* stay, and I won't.
W'h! a feller 'd need the widder's cruse
    T' live back here an' stan' the brunt
Of all expenses, thick and thin —
    Too many men — ain't land enough
T' swing a feller's elbows in, —
    I s'pose you'll take it kind o' rough
But I'm goin' back t'morrer!

It ain't no use t' talk t' me
    Of whut some other feller owns;
I ain't got no grip at all,
    His fire don't warm *my* achin' bones,
An' then I'm ust t' walkin' where
    There ain't no p'lice 'r pavin' stones, —
Of course you'll think I'm mighty sick,
    But I'm goin' back t'morrer!

Fact is, folks, I *love* the West!
    They ain't no other place like home —
They ain't no other place t' *rest*,
    F'r mother 'n me but jest ol' Rome —
Cedar County, up Basswood Run —
    Lived there goin' on thirty years
Come there spring o' sixty-one —
    An' I'm goin' back t'morrer!

I tell ye, things looked purty wild
    On that there prairie then!
We hadn't nary chick n'r child,
    An' we buckled down to work like men.
Handsome land them two claims was
    As ever lay outdoors! Rich an' clean
Of brush an' sloos. Y'r Uncle Daws,
    He used t' say God done his best
On that there land — His level best.

No, I jest can't stand it here,
    Nohow — ain't room to swing my cap.
Ye're all cooped up in this ere flat,
    Jest like chickens in a trap —
I'm mighty sorry, Sue, but I
    Can't stand it, an' mother can't,
If *she* was willing w'y I'd try —
    But I guess we'll go t'morrer.

'N' when we jest get home agin,
    Back t' Cedar County, back t' Rome,
Back t' Basswood Run an' *home*,
    Won't the neighbors jest drop in
When we get settled down, an' grin,
    An' all shake han's — an' Deacon White
Drive up t' laff that laff o' hisn —
    Mother, let's start back t'night!

The corn is jest a-rampin' now,
    I c'n hear the leaves a-russlin'
As they twist an' swing an' bow,

I c'n see the boys a-husslin'
In the medder by the crick,
Forkin' hay f'r all in sight,
An' the birds an' bees s' thick!
O we *must* start back t'night!

AIDGEWISE FEELIN'S

AIDGEWISE FEELIN'S

A FUNERAL is a depressing affair under the best circumstances, but a funeral in a lonely farmhouse in March,
the roads full of slush, the ragged gray clouds leaping
the sullen hills like eagles, is tragic.

The teams arrived splashed with mud, the women
blue with cold under their scanty cotton-quilt lap robes,
their hats set awry by the wind. They scurried into
the house, to sit and shiver in the best room, where all
the chairs that could contrive to stand erect, and all of
any sort that could be borrowed, were crammed in
together to seat the women folks.

The men drove out to the barn, and having blanketed
their teams with lap robes, picked their way through the
slush of the yard over to the lee side of the haystack,
where the pale sun occasionally shone.

They spoke of " diseased " Williams, as if Diseased
were his Christian name. They whittled shingles or
stalks of straw as they talked.

Sooner or later, after each new arrival, they branched
off upon politics, and the McKinley Bill was handled
gingerly. If any one, in his zeal, raised his voice above
a certain pitch, some one said " Hish! " and the new-
comer's voice sank again to that abnormal quiet which
falls now and again on these loud-voiced folk of the
wind and open spaces.

The boys hung around the kitchen and smoke-house, playing sly jokes upon each other in order to provoke that explosion of laughter so thoroughly enjoyed by those who can laugh noiselessly.

A snort of this sort brought Deacon Williams out to reprimand them, " Boys, boys, you should have more respect for the dead."

The preacher came. The choir raised a wailing chant for the dead, but the group by the haystack did not move.

Occasionally they came back, after talking about seeding and the price of hogs, to the discussion of the dead man's affairs.

" I s'pose his property will go to Emmy and Serry, half and half."

" I expec' so. He always said so, an' John wa'n't a man to whiffle about every day."

" Well, Emmy won't make no fuss, but if Ike don't git more'n his half, I'll eat the greaser."

" Who's ex-e*cu*tor ? "

" Deacon Williams, I expect."

" Well, the Deacon's a slick one," some one observed, as if that were an excellent quality in an executor.

" They ain't no love lost between Bill Gray and Harkey, I don't expect."

" No, I don't think they is."

" Ike don't seem to please people. It's queer, too. He tries awful hard."

The voice of the preacher within, raised to a wild shout, interrupted them.

"The Elder's gettin' warmed up," said one of the
story-tellers, pausing in his talk. "And so I told Bill
if he wanted the cord-wood —"

The sun shone warmer, and the chickens *caw-cawed*
feebly. The colts whinnied, and a couple of dogs
rolled and tumbled in wild frolic, while the voice of
the preacher sounded dolefully or in humming mono-
tone.

Meanwhile, in the house, in the best room and in the
best seats near the coffin, the women, in their black,
worn dresses, with wrinkled, sallow faces and gnarled
hands, sat shivering. Theirs was to be the luxury of
the ceremony.

The carpet was damp and muddy, the house was chill,
and the damp wind filled them all with ague ; but they
had so much to see and talk about, that time passed
rapidly. Each one entering was studied critically to
see whether dress and deportment were proper to the
occasion or not, and if one of the girls smiled a little as
she entered, some one was sure to whisper : —

"Heartless thing, how *can* she ?"

There were a few young men, only enough to help
out on the singing, and they remained mainly in the
kitchen where they were seen occasionally in anxious
consultation with Deacon Williams.

The girls looked serious, but a little sly, as if they
could smile if the boys looked their way or if one of
the old women should cough her store teeth out.

Upstairs the family were seated in solemn silence, the
two nieces, Emma and Sarah, and Emma's husband,

Harkey, and Sarah's children — deceased Williams had
no wife.   These people sat in stony immobility, except
when Harkey looked at his watch, and said : —

"Seem slow gitten here."

Occasionally women came up the stairway and flung
themselves upon the necks of the mourning nieces, who
submitted to it without apparent disgust or astonishment,
and sank back into the same icy calm after their visitors
had "straightened their things," and retired to the reserved seats below.

Deacon Williams, small, quick, with sunny blue-gray
eyes belying the gloomy curve of his mouth, was everywhere; arranging for bearers, selecting hymns, conferring
with the family, keeping abstracted old women off the
seats reserved for the mourners, and maintaining an
anxious lookout for the minister.

The Deacon was a distant relative of the dead man,
and it was generally admitted that he "would have a
time of it" in administering upon the estate.

At last the word was whispered about that the Elder
was coming.   Word was sent to the smoke-house and
to the haystack to call the stragglers in.   They came
slowly, and finding the rooms all filled considered themselves absolved from a disagreeable duty, and went back
to the sunny side of the haystack, where they smoked
their pipes in ruminative enjoyment.

The Elder, upon entering, took his place beside the
coffin, the foot of which he used for a pulpit on which
to lay his Bible and his hymn-book.   A noise of whispering, rustling, scraping of feet arose as some old men

crowded in among the women, and then the room became silent.

The Elder took his seat and glanced round upon them all with solemn unrecognizing severity, while the mourners came down the creaking pine stairway in proper order of procedure.

Everybody noticed the luxury of new dresses on the nieces and the new suits on the children. Everybody knew the feeling which led to these extravagances. Death, after all, was a majestic visitor, and money was not to stand in the way of a decent showing. Some of the girls smiled slyly at Isaac's gloves, which were too small and would go only halfway on, a fact he tried to conceal by keeping his hands folded. Each boy was provided with a large new stiff cotton handkerchief, which occupied immense space in outside pockets, crumpled as they were into a rustling ball with cruel salient angles like a Chinese puzzle.

The Elder had attended two funerals that week, and like a jaded actor came lamely to his work. His prayer was not entirely satisfactory to the older people, they had expected a " little more power."

He was a thin-faced man, with weak brown eyes and a mouth like a gopher, that is, with very prominent upper teeth. His black coat was worn and shiny, and hung limply, as if at some other period he had been fatter, or as if it had belonged to some other man.

The choir with instinctive skill had selected a wailing hymn, only slightly higher in development than the chant of the Indians, sweet, plaintive at times, barbaric in its moving cadences. They sang it well, in meditative march, looking out of the windows during its interminable length.

Then the Elder read some passages of the Scripture in his " funeral voice," which was entirely different from his " marriage voice " and his " Sunday voice." It had deep cadences in it and chanting inflections, not unlike the negro preachers or the keeners at Irish wakes.

Then he gave out the hymn, which all joined in singing, rising to their feet with much trouble. After they had settled down again he took out a large carefully ironed handkerchief and laid it on the coffin as who should say, " If you have tears, prepare to shed them now."

The absurdity of all this did not appear to his listeners, though they well knew he cared very little about the dead man, who was a very retiring person.

The Elder on his part understood that his audience was before him for the pleasure of weeping, for the delight of seeing agonized faces and hearing wild grief-laden wailing. They were there to feel the delicious creeping thrill of horror and fear, roused by the presence of the corpse and the near shadow of the hovering angel of death.

The Elder led off by some purely perfunctory remarks about the deceased, about his kindness, and his honesty. This caused the nieces to wipe away a sparse tear or two, and he was encouraged as if by slight applause. He developed as usual the idea that in the midst of life we are in death, that no man can tell when his time

will come. He told two or three grewsome stories of
sudden death. His voice now rose in a wild chant now
sank to a hoarse whisper.

The blowing of noses, low sobbings, and fervent
amens from the old men thickened encouragingly, and
he entered upon more impassioned flights. His voice,
naturally sonorous, deepened in powerful song till the
men seated comfortably on their haunches out by the
haystack could plainly hear his words. "Oh, my
brethren, what will you do in that last day?"

Sarah's boys, without in the least understanding what
it all meant, began to weep also and to use their hand-
kerchiefs, so smooth and shining they were useless as
so much legal-cap writing paper.

Their misery would have been enhanced had they
known that out in the wagon-shed under cover of the
Elder's voice the other boys were having a game of
mummelly peg in the warm, dry ground. Their fresh
young souls laughed at death as the early robins out in
the hedge near by defied the winds of March.

Having harrowed the poor sensation-loving souls as
thoroughly as could be desired, the Elder began the pro-
cess of "letting them down easy." He remembered
that the Lord was merciful; that the deceased could
approach him with confidence; that there was a life
beyond the tomb, a life of eternal rest (the allurement
of all hard-working humanity).

Slowly the snuffling and sobbing ceased, the handker-
chiefs took longer and longer intervals of rest, and when
in conclusion the preacher said, "Let us pray," the old

men looked at each other with fervent satisfaction. " It's been a blessed time — a blessed time! "

The pretty girl who sang the soprano looked very interesting with her wet eyelashes, the tears stopped halfway in their course down her rounded cheek. The closing hymn promised endless peace and rest, but was voiced in the same tragic and hopeless music with which the service opened.

Deacon Williams came out to say, " All parties desiring to view the *remains*, will now have an opportunity." He had the hospitable tone of a host inviting his guests in to dinner.

Viewing the remains was considered a religious duty, and the men from outside, and even the boys from behind the smoke-house, felt constrained to come in and pass in shuddering horror before the still face whose breath did not dim the glass above it. Most of them hurried by the box with only a swift side glance down at the strange thing within.

Then the bearers lifted the coffin and slipped it into the platform-spring wagon, which was backed up to the door. The other teams loaded up, and the procession moved off, down the perilously muddy road toward the village burying-ground.

In this way was John Williams, a hard-working, honorable Welshman, buried. His death furnished forth a sombre, dramatic entertainment such as he himself had ceremoniously attended many times. The funeral trotters whom he had seen at every funeral in the valley were now in at his death, and would be at each other's

death, until the black and yellow earth claimed them
all.

A ceremony almost as interesting to the gossips as
the burial was the reading of the will, to which only
the family were invited. After the return of Emma,
her husband, and Sarah from the cemetery, Deacon
Williams read the dead man's bequests, seated in the
best room, which was still littered with chairs and damp
with mud.

The will was simple and not a surprise to any one.
It gave equal division of all the property to the nieces.

"Well, now, when'll we have the settlement?" asked
the Deacon.

"Just's you say, Deacon," said Emma, meekly.

"Suit yourself," said Harkey; "only it 'ad better
come soon. Sooner the better — seedin's coming on."

"Well, to-morrow is Friday, why not Saturday?"

"All right, Saturday." All agreed.

As Harkey drove off down the road he said to his
wife: "The sooner we have it, the fewer things'll git
carried off. The Deacon don't favor me none, and
Bill Gray is sweet on Serry, and he'll bear watchin'."

The Deacon on his part took his chin in his fist and
looked after Harkey. "Seemed a little bit anxious,
'cordin' to *my* notion," he said, with a smile.

II

SATURDAY was deliciously warm and springlike, the
hens woke in the early dawn with a jocund note in

their throats, and the young cattle frisked about the barn-yard, moved to action by the electrical influences of the south wind.

"Clear as a bell overhead," Deacon Williams said.

But Jack Dunlap, Sarah's hand, said, "Nobody travels that way."

Long before dawn the noise of the melting water could be heard running with musical tinkle under the ice. The ponds crashed and boomed in long reverberating explosions, as the sinking water heaved it up and let it fall with crackling roar; flights of ducks flashed over, cackling breathlessly as they scurried straight into the north.

Deacon and Sarah arrived early and took possession, for Sarah was to have the eighty which included the house. They were busy getting things ready for the partition. The Deacon, assisted by Jack, the hired man, was busy hauling the machinery out of the shed into the open air, while Sarah and a couple of neighbors' girls, with skirts tucked up and towels on their heads, were scouring up pots and pans and dusting furniture in the kitchen.

The girls, strong and handsome in their unsapped animal vigor, enjoyed the innocent display of their bare arms and petticoats.

People from Sand Lake passing by wondered what was going on. Gideon Turner had the courage to pull up and call out, for the satisfaction of his wife: —

"What's going on here this fine morning?"

"Oh, we're goin' to settle up the estate!" said Sarah. "Why! how de do, Mrs. Turner?"

" W'y, it's you, is it, Serry ? "

" Yes; it's me, — what they is left of me.   I been here sence six o'clock.   I'm getting things ready for the division.   Deacon Williams is the ex-e*cu*tor, you know."

" Aha !   Less see, you divide equally, I hear."

" Near's we can get at it.   Uncle left me the house eighty, and the valley eighty to Emmy.   Deacon's goin' to parcel out the belongin's."

Turner looked sly.   " How'd Harkey feel ? "

Sarah smiled.   " I don't know and care less.   He'll make trouble if he can, but I don't see how he can.   He agreed to have the Deacon do the dividin', and he'll have to stand by it so far as I can see."

Mrs. Turner looked dubious.   " Well, you know Ike Harkey.   He looks as though sugar wouldn't melt in his mouth, but I tell you I'd hate to have dealin's with him."

Turner broke in: " Well, we must be movin'.   I s'pose you'll move right in ? "

" Yes.   Just as soon's as this thing's settled."

" Well, good-by.   Come up."

" You come down."

Sarah was a heavy, good-natured woman, a widow with " a raft of children."   Probably for that reason her uncle had left her the house, which was large and comfortable.   As she stood looking down the road, one of the girls came out to the gate.   She was a plump, strong creature, a neighbor's girl who had volunteered to help.

" Anybody coming ? "
Q

"Yes. I guess — no, it's going the other way. Ain't it a nice day?"

That was as far as she could carry the utterance of her feeling, but all the morning she had felt the wonderful power of the air. The sun had risen incredibly warm. The wind was in the south, and the crackling, booming roar of ice in the ponds and along the river was like winter letting go its iron grip upon the land. Even the old cows shook their horns, and made comical attempts to frisk with the yearlings. Sarah knew it was foolish, but she felt like a girl that morning — and Bill was coming up the road.

In the midst of the joy of the spring day stood the house, desolate and empty, out of which its owner had been carried to a bed in the cold, clinging clay of the little burying-ground.

The girls and Sarah worked swiftly, brushing, cleaning, setting aside, giving little thought to even the beauty of the morning, which entered their blood unconsciously.

"Well, how goes it?" asked a quick, jovial voice.

The girls gave screams of affected fright.

"Why, Deacon! You nearly scared the life out of us."

Deacon Williams was always gallant.

"I didn't know I was given to scaring the ladies," he said. "Well, who's here?"

"Nobody but us so far."

"Hain't seen nothing o' Harkey?"

"Not a thing. He sent word he'd be on hand, though."

"M—, well, we've got the machinery invoiced. Guess I'll look around and kind o' get the household things in my mind's eye," said the Deacon, taking on the air of a public functionary.

"All right. We'll have everything ready here in a few minutes."

They returned to work, dusting and scrubbing. The girls with their banter put death into the background as an obscure and infrequent incident of old age.

Sarah again studied the road down the Coolly.

"Well there! I see a team coming up the Coolly now; wonder if it's Emmy."

"Looks more like Bill Gray's team," said one of the girls, looking slyly at Sarah, who grew very red.

"Oh, you're too sharp, ain't you?"

It was perfectly ridiculous (to the young people) to see these middle-aged lovers courting like sixteen-year-olds, and they had no mercy on either Bill or Sarah.

Bill drove up in leisurely way, his horses steaming, his wagon-wheels loaded with mud. Mrs. Gray was with him, her jolly face shining like the morning sun.

"Hello, folkses, are you all here?"

"Good morning, Mrs. Gray," said the Deacon, approaching to help her out. "Hello, Bill, nice morning."

Bill looked at Sarah for a moment. "Bully good," he said, leaving his mother to scramble down the wagon-wheel alone — at least so far as he was concerned, but the Deacon stood below courageously.

Mrs. Gray cried out in her loud good humor: "Look out, Deacon, don't git too near me — if I should fall on you there wouldn't be a grease spot left. *There!* I'm all right now," she said, having reached ground without accident.   She shook her dress and looked briskly around.   " Wal, what you done, anyway ?   Emmy's folks come yet ? "

" No, but I guess that's them comin' now.   I hope Ike won't come, though."

Mrs. Gray stared at the Deacon.   " Why not ? "

" Well, he's just sure to make a fuss," said Jack, " he's so afraid he won't get his share."

Bill chewed on a straw and looked at Sarah abstractedly.

" Well, what's t' be done ? " inquired Mrs. Gray, after a pause.

" Can't do much till Emmy gets here," said Sarah.

" Oh, I guess we can.   Bill, you put out y'r team, we won't get away 'fore dinner."

The men drove off to the barn, leaving the women to pick their way on chips and strips of board laid in the mud, to the safety of the chip-pile, and thence to the kitchen, which was desolately littered with utensils.

Deacon assumed command with the same alertness, and with the same sunny gleam in his eye, with which he directed the funeral a few days before.

" Now, Bill, put out your team and help Jack and me pen them hogs.   Women folks 'll git things ready here."

Emma came at last, driven by Harkey's brother and his hired man.   They were both brawny fellows, rude and irritable, and the Deacon lifted his eyebrows and whistled when he saw them drive in with a lumber wagon.

The women swarmed out to greet Emma, who was a thin, irritable, feeble woman.

" Better late than never. Where's Ike?" inquired Mrs. Gray.

" Well, he — couldn't git away very well — he's got t' clean up some seed-oats," she answered nervously. After the men drove off, however, she added: " He thought he hadn't ought to come; he didn't want to cause no aidgewise feelin's, so he thought he hadn't better come — he'd just leave it to you, Deacon."

The Deacon said, " All right, all right! We'll fix it up!" but he didn't feel so sure of it after that, though he set to work bravely.

The sun, growing warmer, fell with pleasant gleam around the kitchen door and around the chip-pile where the hens were burrowing. The men worked in their shirt-sleeves.

" Well, now, we'll share the furniture an' stuff next," said the Deacon, looking around upon his little interested semicircle of spectators. " Now, put Emmy's things over there and Serry's things over here. I'll call 'em off, and, if they's no objection, you girls can pass 'em over."

He cleared his throat and began in the voice of one in authority : —

" Thirteen pans, six to Emmy, seven to Serry;" then hastened to add: " I'll balance that by giving the biggest of the two kittles to Emmy. Rollin' pin and cake board to Serry, two flat-irons to Emmy, small tub to Emmy, large one to Serry, balanced by the tin water pail. Dozen clo'se-pins; half an' half, six o' one, half-dozen t'other," he said with a smile at his own joke, while the others actively placed the articles in separate piles.

"Stove to Serry, because she has the house, bureau to Emmy."

At this point Mrs. Gray said, "I guess that ain't quite even, Deacon; the bureau ain't worth much."

"Oh, no, no, that's all right! Let her have it," Emma protested nervously.

"Give her an extry tick, anyway," said Sarah, not to be outdone in magnanimity.

"Settle that between ye," said the Deacon.

He warmed to his work now, and towels, pans, crockery, brooms, mirrors, pillows, and bedticks were rapidly set aside in two groups on the soft soil. The poverty of the home could best be seen in the display of its pitiful furniture.

The two nieces looked on impassively, standing side by side. The men came to move the bureau and other heavy things and looked on, while the lighter things were being handed over by Mrs. Gray and the girls.

At noon they sat down in the empty kitchen and ate a cold snack — at least, the women took seats, the men stood around and lunched on hunks of boiled beef and slices of bread. There was an air of constraint upon the male portion of the party not shared by Mrs. Gray and the girls.

"Well, that settles things in the house," beamed the Deacon as he came out with the women trailing behind him; "an' now in about two jerks of a dead lamb's tail, we'll git at the things out in the barn."

"Wal, we don't know much about machines and things, but I guess we'd better go out and keep you men from fightin'," said Mrs. Gray, shaking with fun; "Ike didn't come because he didn't want to make any trouble, but I guess he might just as well 'a' come as send two such critters as Jim 'n' Hank."

The women laughed at her frankness, and in very good humor they all went out to the barn-yard.

"Now, these things can't be laid out fast as I call 'em off, but we'll do the best we can."

"Let's try the stawk first," said Jim.

The women stood around with shawls pinned over their heads while the division of the stock went forward. The young men came often within chaffing distance of the girls.

There were nine shotes nearly of a size, and the Deacon said, "I'll give Serry the odd shote."

"Why so?" asked Jim Harkey, a sullen-faced man of thirty.

"Because a shote is hard to carry off and I can balance — "

"Well, I guess you can balance f'r Em 'bout as well as f'r Serry."

The Deacon was willing to yield a point. "Any objection, Bill? If not, why — "

"Nope, let her go," said Bill.

"What 'ave *you* got to say 'bout it?" asked Jim, insolently.

Bill turned his slow bulk. "I guess I've a good 'eal to say — haven't I, Serry?"

Sarah reddened, but stood beside him bravely. "I guess you have, Bill, about as much as *I* have." There was a moment of dramatic tension and the girls tingled with sympathy.

"Let 'er go," said Bill, splitting a straw with his knife. He had not proposed to Sarah before and he felt an unusual exaltation to think it came so easy after all.

When they reached the cattle, Jim objected to striking a balance with a "farrer cow," and threw the Deacon's nice calculation all out of joint.

"Let it go, Jim," pleaded Emma.

"I won't do it," Ike said — I mean I know he don't want no farrer cow, he's got two now."

The Deacon was a little nettled. "I guess that's going to stand," he said sharply.

Jim swore a little but gave in, and came back with an access of ill humor on a division of the horses.

"But I've give you the four heavy horses to balance the four others and the two-year-old," said the Deacon.

"I'll be damned if I stand that," said Jim.

"I guess you'll have to," said the Deacon.

Emma pleaded, "Let it go, Jim, don't make a fuss."

Jim raged on, "I'll be cawn-demmed if I'll stand it. I don't — Ike don't want them spavined old crows; they're all ring-boned and got the heaves." His long repressed ill-nature broke out.

"Toh, toh!" said the Deacon, "Don't kick over the traces now. We'll fix it up some way."

Emma tried to stop Jim, but he shook her off and continued to walk back and forth behind the horses munching on quietly, unconscious of any dispute about their value.

Bill sat on the oat box in his hulking way, his heels thumping a tune, his small gray eyes watching the angry man.

"Don't make a darn fool of yourself," he said placidly.

Jim turned, glad of the chance for a row, "You better keep out of this."

Bill continued to thump, the palms of his big hands resting on the edge of the box. "I'm in it," he said conclusively.

"Well, you git out of it! I ain't goin' to be bull-dozed — that ain't what I come here for."

"No, I see it ain't," said Bill. "If you're after a row you can have it right here. You won't find a better place."

"There, there," urged the Deacon. "What's the use? Keep cool and don't tear your shirts."

Mrs. Gray went up to Jim and took him by the arm. "You need a good spankin' to make you good-natured," she said. "I think the Deacon has done first rate, and you ought 'o —"

"Let go o' me," he snarled, raising his hand as if to strike her.

Bill's big boot lunged out, catching Harkey in the ribs,

and if the Deacon had not sprung to his assistance Jim would have been trampled to pieces by the scared horse under whose feet he found himself. He was wild with dizzy, breathless rage.

"Who hit me?" he demanded.

Bill's shapeless hulk straightened up and stood beside him as if his pink flesh had suddenly turned to oak. Out of his fat cheeks his gray eyes glared.

"I did. Want another?"

The Deacon and Jack came between and prevented the encounter which would have immediately followed. Bill went on: —

"They cain't no man lay a hand on my mother and live long after it." He was thoroughly awake now. There was no slouch to his action at that moment, and Jim was secretly pleased to have the encounter go by.

"You come here for a fuss and you can have it, both of you," Bill went on in unusual eloquence. "Deacon's tried to do the square thing, Emmy's tried to do the square thing, and Serry's kep' quiet, but you've been sour and ugly the whole time, and now it's goin' to stop."

"This ain't the last of this thing," said Jim.

"You never'll have a better time," said Bill.

Mrs. Gray and the Deacon turned in now to quiet Bill, and the settlement went on. Jim kept close watch on the proceedings, and muttered his dissent to his friends, but was careful not to provoke Bill further.

In dividing the harnesses they came upon a cow-bell hanging on a nail. The Deacon jingled it as he passed.

" Goes with the bell-cow," he said, and nothing further was said of it. Jim apparently did not consider it worth quarrelling about.

At last the work was done, a terribly hard day's work. The machines and utensils were piled in separate places, the cattle separated, and the grain measured. As they were about to leave, the Deacon said finally : —

" If there's any complaint to make, let's have it right now. I want this settlement to *be* a settlement. Is everybody satisfied ? "

" I am," said Emmy. " Ain't you, Serry ? "

" Why, of course," said Sarah, who was a little slower of speech. " I think the Deacon has done first rate. I ain't a word of fault to find, have you, Bill ? "

" Nope, not an ioty," said Bill, readily.

Jim did not agree in so many words, but, as he said nothing, the Deacon ended : —

" Well, that settles it. It ain't goin' to rain, so you can leave these things right here till Monday. I guess I'll be gettin' out for home. Good evening, everybody."

Emma drove away down the road with Jim, but Sarah remained to straighten up the house. Harkey's hired hand went home with Dade Walker who considered that walk the pleasant finish to a very interesting day's work. She sympathized for the time with the Harkey faction.

Sunday forenoon, when Bill and Sarah drove up to the farm to put things in order in the house, they found Ike Harkey walking around with that queer side glance he had, studying the piles of furniture, and mentally weighing the pigs.

He greeted them smoothly : " Yes, yes, I'm *purr*fickly satisfied, *purr*fickly !   Not a word to say — better'n I expected," he added.

Bill was not quite keen enough to perceive the insult which lay in that final clause, and Sarah dared not inform him for fear of trouble.

As Harkey drove away, however, Bill had a dim feeling of dissatisfaction with him.

" He's too gol-dang polite, that feller is ; I don't like such butter-mouth chaps — they'd steal the cents off'n a dead nigger's eyes."

III

THE second Sunday after the partition of goods the entire Coolly turned out to church in spite of the muddy road.   The men, after driving up to the door of the little white church and helping the women to alight, drove out to the sheds along the fence and gathered in knots beside their wagons in the warm spring sun.   It was very pleasant there, and the men leaned with relaxed muscles upon the wagon-wheels, or sat on the fence with jack-knives in hand.   The horses, weary with six days seeding, slept with closed eyes and drooping lips. Generally the talk was upon spring work, each man bragging of the number of acres he had sown during the week, but this morning the talk was all about the division which had come between the nieces of " deceased Williams."   They discussed it slowly as one might eat a choice pudding in order to extract the flavor from each spoonful.

"What is it all about, anyhow?" asked Jim Cranby. "I ain't heard nothing about it." He had stood in open-mouthed perplexity trying to catch a clew. Coming late, he found it baffling.

"That shows where he lives; a man might as well live in a well as up in Molasses Gap," said one of the younger men, pointing up to the Coolly. "Why, Ike Harkey is kicking about the six shotes the Deacon put off on him."

"No, it wasn't the shotes, it was a farrer cow," put in Clint Stone.

"Well, *I* heard it was a shote."

"So did I," said another.

"Well, Bill Gray told Jinks Ike had stole a cow-bell that belonged to the black farrer cow," said another late comer.

"Stole a cow-bell," and they all drew closer together. This was really worth while!

"Yes, sir; Jinks told me he heard Bill say so yesterday. That's the way I heard it."

"Well, I'll be cussed, if that ain't small business for Ike Harkey!"

"How did it happen?" asked Cranby, with sharpened appetite.

"Well, I didn't hear no p'rtic'lars, but it seems the bell was hangin' on a peg in the barn, and when they got home from church it was gone, hide an' hair. Bill is dead sure Ike took it."

"Say, there'll be fun over that yet, won't they," said one of the fellows, with a grin.

"Well, Ike better keep out of Bill's way, that's all."

"Well — I ain't takin' sides. Some young'un may have took it."

"Well, let's go in, boys; I see the Elder's come. By gum, there's Harkey!" They all looked toward Harkey, who had just driven up to the door.

Harkey came into church holding his smooth, serious face a little one side, in his usual way, quiet and dignified, as if he were living up to his Sunday suit of clothes. He seemed to be unconscious of the attitude in which he stood toward most of his neighbors.

Bill and Sarah were not present, and that gave additional color to the story of trouble between the sisters.

After the sermon Deacon Harkey led the Sunday School, and the critics of his action were impressed more than usual with his smooth and quiet utterance. Emma seemed more than ordinarily worn and dispirited.

It was perfectly natural that Mrs. Gray should be the last person to know of the division which had slowly set in between the two sisters and their factions. Charitable and guileless herself, it was difficult for her to conceive of slander and envy.

Nevertheless, a division had come about, slowly, but decisively. The entire Coolly was involved in the discussion before Mrs. Gray gave it any serious attention, but one day, when Sarah came in upon her and poured out a mingled flood of sorrow and invective, the good soul was aghast.

" Well, well, I swan ! There, there ! I wouldn't make so much fuss over it ! " she said, stripping her hands out of the biscuit dough in order to go over and pat Sarah on the shoulder. " After all that to-do gettin' settled, seems 's if you ought 'o *stay* settled. Good land ! It ain't anything to have a fuss over, any-way ! "

" But it is *our* cow-bell. It belonged on the black farrer cow, that Jim turned his nose up at, and he sneaked around and got it just to spite us."

" Oh, I guess not," she replied incredulously.

" Well, he did ; and Emmy put him up to it, and I know she did," said Sarah in a lamentable voice.

" Sary Ann," said Mrs. Gray, as sharply as any one ever heard her speak, " that's a pretty way to talk about your sister, ain't it ? "

" Well, Mrs. Jim Harkey said — "

" You never mind what Mrs. Jim Harkey said ; she's a *snoop* and everybody knows it."

" But she wouldn't tell that, if it weren't so."

" Well, I tell you, I wouldn't pay no attention to what she said, and I wouldn't make such a fuss over an old cow-bell, anyway."

" But the cow-bell is only the starting point ; she ain't been near the house since, and she says all kinds of mean, nasty things about us."

" All comes through Mrs. Jim, I suppose," said Mrs. Gray, with some sarcasm.

" No, it don't. She told Dade Walker that I got all the biggest flat-irons, when she knows I offered her the bureau. I did everything I could to make her feel satisfied."

"I know you did, and now you must just keep cool till I see Emmy myself."

When Mrs. Gray started out on her mission of pacification, she found it to be entirely out of her control. The Coolly was actively partisan. One party stood by the Harkeys, and another took Sarah's part, while the *tertium quid* said it was "all darn foolishness."

Mrs. Gray was appalled at the state of affairs, but struggled to maintain a neutral position. In May, when Bill and Sarah were married, things had reached such a stage that Emma was not invited to the wedding supper. Nothing could have cut deeper than this neglect, and thereafter adherents of the third remove declined to speak when passing; some even refused to nod. The Harkey faction also condemned the early marriage of Bill and Sarah as unseemly.

Soon after, Emma came again to see Mrs. Gray, salty with tears, and crushed with the slight Sarah had put upon her. She was a plain pale woman, anyway, and weeping made her pitiable. She explained the situation with her head on Mrs. Gray's lap : —

"She never has been to see me since that day, and — but I hoped she'd come and see me, but she never sent me any invitation to her wedding." She choked with sobs at the memory of it.

Mrs. Gray realized the enormity of the offence, and she could only put her arms around Emma's back and say, "There, there, I wouldn't take on so about it." As a matter of fact, she had striven to have Bill send an invitation to his brother-in-law, but Bill was inflexible on that point. With the sound of the stolen cow-bell ringing in his ears, he could not bring himself to ask Ike Harkey into his house.

After Emma grew a little calmer, Mrs. Gray tried again to bridge the chasm. "Now, I just believe if you would go to Sarah —"

"I can't do that! She'd slam the door in my face. Jim's wife says Sarah said I shouldn't pick a single currant out of the garden this year!"

"I don't go much on what Jim's wife says," put in Mrs. Gray, guardedly. She had begun to feel that Jim's wife was the main disturbing element.

The sisters really suffered from their separation. They had been so used to running in at all times of the day that each missed the other wofully. It had been their habit whenever they needed each other to help cook, or cut a dress, to hang a cloth out of the chamber window, a sign which was sure to bring help post-haste; but now nothing would induce either of them to make the first concession.

Two or three times when Emma, feeling especially lonely, was on the point of hanging out the signal, she was prevented by the thought of some cruel message Mrs. Jim had brought. Jim lived on Ike's farm in a small house that had been Emma's first home, and Mrs. Jim was almost as much in her house as in her own. She had no children, and was a mischief-maker, not so much from ill will as from a love of dramatic situations;

R

it was her life, this dramatic play of loves and hates among her friends and neighbors.

Emma feared her husband, too; he was so self-contained, and so inexorably moral, at least in appearance. He sweetly said he bore no ill will toward the Grays, but he must insist that his wife should not visit them until they apologized. He took the matter very serenely, however.

The sound of the cow-bell was a constant daily irritation to Bill; he was slow to wrath, but the bell seemed to rasp on his tenderest nerve; it had a curiously exultant sound heard in the early morning — it seemed to voice Harkey's triumph. Bill's friends were astonished at the change in him. He grew dark and thunderous with wrath whenever Harkey's name was mentioned.

One day Ike's cattle broke out of the pasture into Bill's young oats, and though Ike hurried after them, it seemed to Bill he might have got them out a little quicker than he did. He said nothing then, however, but when a few days later they broke in again, he went over there in very bad humor.

" I want this thing stopped," he said.

Ike was mending the fence. He smiled in his sweet way, and said smoothly, " I'm sorry, but when they once git a taste of grain it's pretty hard to keep 'em — "

" Well, there ought to be a new fence here," said Bill. " That fence is as rotten as a pumpkin."

" I s'pose they had; yes, sir, that's so," Harkey assented quickly. " I'm ready to build my half, you know," he said, " any time — any time you are."

"Well, I'll build mine to-morrow," said Bill. "I can't have your cattle pasturing on my oats."

"All right, all right. I'll have mine done as quick as yourn."

"Well, see't you do; I don't want my grain all tramped into the ground and I ain't a-goin' to have it."

Harkey hastily gathered up his tools, saying, "Yes, yes, all right."

"You might send home that cow-bell of mine while you're about it," Bill called after him, but Harkey did not reply or turn around.

IV

THE line fence ran up the bluff toward the summit of the ridge to the east. On each side it was set with smooth green slopes of pasture and pleasant squares of wheat, until it reached the woods and ran under the oaks and walnuts and birches to the cliffs of lichen-spotted stone which topped the summit.

Bill walked the full length of the fence to see how much of the old material could be used. He recognized the bell on one of Harkey's cattle, and he grew wrathful at the sight of another cow peacefully gnawing the fresh, green grass, with the bell, which belonged to the black cow, on her neck.

It was mid-spring. Everywhere was the vivid green of the Wisconsin landscape; the slopes were like carefully tended lawns, without stumps or stones; the groves rose up the hills, pink and gray and green in softly rounded billows of cherry bloom and tender oak and elm foliage. Here and there under the forest tender plants and flowers had sprung up, slender and succulent like all productions of a rich and shadowed soil.

Early the next morning Bill and his two hands began to work in the meadow, working toward the ridge; Harkey and his brother and their hands began at the ridge and worked down toward the meadow; each party could hear the axes of the other ringing in the still, beautiful spring air.

Bill's hired hand, on his way to the spring about the middle of the forenoon, met Jim Harkey, who said wickedly in answer to a jocular greeting : —

" Don't give me none of your lip now; we'll break your necks for two cents."

The hand came to Bill with the story. " Bill, they're on the fight."

" Oh, I guess not."

" Well, they be. We better not run up against them to-day if we don't want trouble."

" Well, I ain't goin' to dodge 'em," said Bill; " I ain't in that business; if they want fight, we'll accommodate 'em with the best we've got in the shop."

At noon, Harkey's gang went to dinner a little earlier, and, as they came down the path quite near, Jim said with a sneer : —

" You managed to git the easiest half of the fence, didn't yeh ? "

" We took the half that belongs to us," said Bill. " *We* don't take what don't belong to us."

" Cow-bells, for instance," put in Bill's hired hand, with a provoking intonation.

Jim stopped and his face twisted with rage; Ike paused a little farther on down the path. Jim came closer.

" Say, I know what you're driving at and you're a liar, and for a leather cent I'd lick you like hell!"

" You can't do it. You don't weigh enough."

" Oh, shut up, Jack," called Bill. " Go about y'r business," he said to Jim, " or I'll take a hand."

Jim's face flamed into a wild wrath. His lips lifted at the corners like a wolf's as he leaped the fence with a wild spring and lunged against Bill's breast. The larger man went down, but his great arms closed about his assailant's neck with a bear-like grip. Jim could neither rise nor strike; with a fury no animal could equal he pressed his hands upon Bill's throat and thrust his elbow into his mouth in the attempt to strangle him. He meant murder.

Jack faced the other men, who came running up. Ike seized a stake, and was about to leap over, when Jack raised an axe in the air.

" Stand off!" he yelled, and his voice rang through the woods; he noticed how harsh and wild it sounded in the silence. He heard a grunting sound, and gave one glance at the two men writhing amid the ferns silent as grappling bull-dogs.

Bill had fallen in the brake and seemed wedged in. At last there came into his heart a terrible shiver, a blind desperation that uncoiled all the strength in his great bulk. Then he seemed to bound from the ground, as he twisted the other man under him, and shook himself free.

He dragged one great maul of a fist free and drove it at the face beneath him. Jim saw it coming and turned his head. The blow fell on his neck and his carnivorous grin smoothed out as if sleep had suddenly fallen upon him. He drew a long, shuddering breath, his muscles quivered, and his clenched hands fell open.

Bill rose upon his knees and looked at him. A deep awe fell upon him. In the pause he heard the robins rioting from the trees in the lower valley, and the woodpecker cried resoundingly.

" You've killed him! " cried Ike, as he climbed hastily over the fence.

Bill did not reply. The men faced each other in solemn silence, all wish for murder going out of their hearts. The sobbing cry of the mourning dove, which they had been hearing all day, suddenly assumed new meaning.

" *Ah, woe, woe is me!* " it cried.

" Bring water! " shouted Ike, kneeling beside his brother.

Bill knelt there with him, while the rest dashed water upon Jim's face.

At last he began to breathe like a fretful, waking child, and looking up into the scared faces above him, motioned the water away from him. The angry look came back into his face, but it was mixed with perplexity.

He touched his hand to his face and brought it down covered with blood. "How much am I hurt?" he said fiercely.

"Oh, nothing much," Ike hastened to say; "it's just a scratch."

Jim struggled to his elbow and looked around him. It all seemed to come back to him. "Did he do it fair?" he demanded of his companions.

"Oh, yes; it was fair enough," said Ike.

Jim looked at Jack. "That *thing* didn't hit me with his axe, did he?"

Jack grinned. "No, but I was just a-goin' to when Bill belted you one," was the frank and convincing reply.

Jim got up slowly and faced Bill. "Well, that settles it; it's all right! You're a better man than I am. That's all I've got to say."

He climbed back over the fence and led the way down to dinner without looking back.

"What give ye that lick on the side o' the head, Jim?" his wife asked, when he sat down at the dinner-table.

"Never you mind," he replied surlily, but he added, "Ike's axe come off, and give me a side-winder."

Bill carefully removed all marks of his struggle and walked into dinner shamefacedly, all muscle gone out of his bulk of fat. His sudden return to primeval savagery grew monstrous in the cheerful kitchen, with its noise of hearty children, sizzling meat, and the clatter of dishes.

The stove was not drawing well and Sarah did not notice anything out of the way with Bill.

"I never see such a hateful thing in all my life," she said, referring to the stove. "That rhubarb duff won't be fit for a hog to eat; the undercrust ain't baked the least bit yet, and I have had it in there since fifteen minutes after 'leven."

Bill said generously, "Oh, well, never mind, Serry; we'll worry it down some way."

V

ALL through July and August Mrs. Jim Harkey seemed to renew her endeavors to keep the sisters apart; she still carried spiteful tales to and fro, amplifying them with an irresistible histronic tendency. It had become a matter of self-exoneration with her then. She could not stop now without seeming to admit she had been mischief-making in the past. If the sisters should come together, her lies would instantly appear.

Emma grew morose, irritable, and melancholy; she was suffering for her sister's wholesome presence, and yet, being under the dominion of the mischief-maker, dared not send word or even mention the name of her sister in the presence of the Harkeys.

Mrs. Jim came up to the house to stay as Emma got too ill to work, and took charge of the house. The children hated her fiercely, and there were noisy battles in the kitchen constantly wearing upon the nerves of the sick woman who lay in the restricted gloom of the sitting room bed-chamber, within hearing of every squall.

There were moments of peace only when Ike was in the house. Smooth as he was, Jim's wife was afraid of him. There was something compelling in his low-toned voice; his presence subdued but did not remove strife.

His silencing of the tumult hardly arose out of any consideration for his wife, but rather from his inability to enjoy his paper while the clamor of war was going on about him.

He was not a tender man, and yet he prided himself on being a very calm and even-tempered man. He kept out of Bill's way, and considered himself entirely justified in his position regarding the cow-bell. It is doubtful if he would have accepted an apology.

Emma suffered acutely from Mrs. Harkey's visits. Something mean and wearying went out from her presence, and her sharp, bold face was a constant irritation. Sometimes when she thought herself alone, Emma crawled to the window which looked up the Coolly, toward Sarah's home, and sat there silently longing to send out a cry for help. But at the sound of Jane Harkey's step she fled back into bed like a frightened child.

She became more and more childish and more flighty in her thoughts as her time of trial drew near, and she became more subject to her jailer. She grew morbidly silent, and her large eyes were restless and full of pleading.

One day she heard Mrs. Smith talking out in the kitchen.

"How is Emmy to-day, Mrs. Jim?"

"Well, not extry. She ain't likely to come out as well as usual this time, I don't think," was the brutally incautious reply; "she's pretty well run down, and I wouldn't be surprised if she had some trouble."

"I suppose Sarah will be down to help you," said Mrs. Smith.

"Well, I guess not — not after what she's told."

"What has she told?" asked Mrs. Smith, in her sweet and friendly voice.

"Why, she said she wouldn't set foot in this house if we all *died*."

"I never heard her say that, and I don't believe she ever *did* say it," said Mrs. Smith, firmly.

Emma's heart glowed with a swift rush of affection toward her sister and Mrs. Smith; she wanted to cry out her faith in Sarah, but she dared not.

Mrs. Harkey slammed the oven door viciously. "Well, you can believe it or not, just as you like; I heard her say it."

"Well, I didn't, so I can't believe it."

When Mrs. Smith came in, Emma was ready to weep, so sweet and cheery was her visitor's face.

She found no chance to talk with her, however, for Mrs. Harkey kept near them during her visit. Once, while Mrs. Jim ran out to look at the pies, Mrs. Smith whispered: "Don't you believe what they say about Sarah. She's just as kind as can be — I know she is.

She's looking down this way every day, and I know she'd come down instanter if you'd send for her. I'm going up that way, and — "

She found no further chance to say anything, but from that moment Emma began to think of letting Sarah know how much she needed her. She planned to hang out the cloth as she used to. She exaggerated its importance in the way of an invalid, until it attained the significance of an act of treason. She felt like a criminal even in thinking about it.

Several times in the night she dreamed she had put the cloth out and that Jim and his wife had seen it and torn it down. She awoke two or three times to find herself sitting up in bed staring out of the window, through which the moon shone and the multitudinous sounds of the mid-summer insects came sonorously.

Once her husband said, "What's the matter? it seems to me you'd rest better if you'd lay down and keep quiet." His voice was low enough, but it had a peculiar inflection, which made her sink back into bed by his side, shivering with fear and weeping silently.

The next day Jim and her husband both went off to town, and Jim's wife, after about ten o'clock, said : —

"Now, Emmy, I'm going down to Smith's to get a dress pattern, and I want you to keep quiet right here in bed. I'll be right back; I'll set some water here, and I guess you won't want anything else until I get back. I'll run right down and right back."

After hearing the door close, Emma lay for a few

minutes listening, waiting until she felt sure Mrs. Harkey was well out of the yard, then she crept out of bed and crawled to the window. Mrs. Jim was far down the road; she could see her blue dress and her pink sunbonnet.

The sick woman seized the sheet and pulled it from the bed; the clothes came with it, but she did not mind that. She pulled herself painfully up the stairway and across the rough floor of the chamber to the window which looked toward her sister's house, and with a wild exultation flung the sheet far out and dropped on her knees beside the open window.

She moaned and cried wildly as she waved the sheet. The note of a scared child was in her voice.

"Oh, Serry, come quick! Oh, I *need* you, Serry! I didn't mean to be mean; I want to see you *so!* Oh, dear, oh, dear! Oh, Serry, come quick!"

Then space and the world slipped away, and she knew nothing of time again until she heard the anxious voice of Sarah below.

"Emmy, where *are* you, Emmy?"

"Here I be, Serry."

With swift, heavy tread Sarah hurried up the stairs, and the dear old face shone upon her again; those kind gray eyes full of anxiety and of love.

Emma looked up like a child entreating to be lifted. Her look so pitifully eager went to the younger sister's maternal heart.

"You poor, dear soul! Why didn't you send for me before?"

"Oh, Serry, don't leave me again, will you?"

When Mrs. Harkey returned she found Sarah sitting by Emma's side in the bed-chamber. Sarah looked at her with all the grimness her jolly fat face could express.

"You ain't needed *here*," she said coldly. "If you want to do anything, find a man and send him for the Doctor — quick. If she dies you'll be her murderer."

Mrs. Harkey was subdued by the bitterness of accusation in Sarah's face as well as by Emma's condition. She hurried down the Coolly and sent a boy wildly galloping toward the town. Then she went home and sat down by her own hearthstone feeling deeply injured.

When the Doctor came he found a poor little boy baby crying in Sarah's arms. It was Emma's seventh child, but the ever sufficing mother-love looked from her eyes undimmed, limitless as the air.

"Will it live, Doctor? It's so little," she said, with a sigh.

"Oh, yes, I suppose so!" said the Doctor, as if its living were not entirely a blessing to itself or others. "Yes, I've seen lots of lusty children begin life like that. But," he said to Sarah at the door, "she needs better care than the babe!"

"She'll git it," said Sarah, with deep solemnity, "if I have to move over here — and live."

GROWING OLD

F'R forty years next Easter day,
   Him and me in wind and weather
Have been a-gittin' bent 'n' gray,
   Moggin' along together.

We're not so *very* old, of course,
   But still, we ain't so awful spry
As when we went to singin'-school
   Afoot and 'cross lots, him and I,
And walked back home the longest way;
   An' the moon a-shinin' on the snow,
Makin' the road as bright as day,
   An' his voice soundin' low.

Land sakes !   Jest hear me talk,
   F'r all the world jest like a girl,
Me — nearly sixty !   Well — awell !
   I *was* so tall and strong, the curl
In my hair, Sim said, was like
   The crinkles in a medder brook,
So brown and bright, but there !
   I guess he got *that* from a book.

His talk in them there days was full
   Of jest such nonsense — don't you think
I didn't like it, for I did;
   I walked along there, glad to drink
His words in like the breath o' life,

Heavens and earth, what fools we women be!
And when he asked me for his wife,
    I answered " Yes," of course, y' see.

An' then come work, and trouble bit —
    Not much time for love talk then.
We bought a farm and mortgaged it,
    And worked and slaved like all possessed
To lift that turrible grindin' weight.
    I washed and churned and sewed,
An' childrun come, till we had eight;
    As han'some babes as ever growed
To walk beside a mother's knee,
They helped me bear it all, y' see.

It ain't been nothin' else but scrub,
    An' rub, and bake, and stew
The hull, hull time, over stove or tub;
    No time to rest as men folks do.
I tell yeh, sometimes I sit and think
    How nice the grave 'll be, jest
    One nice, sweet, everlastin' rest!

O don't look scart! I mean
    Jest what I say. Ain't crazy yet,
But it's enough to make me so.
    Of course it ain't no use to fret,
Who said it was? It's nacherl, though,
    But, O if I was only there
In the past, and young once more,

An' had the crinkles in my hair,
An' arms as round and strong, and side
    As it was then!   I'd — I'd —

I'd do it all over again like a fool,
    I s'pose!   I'd take the pain,
An' work, an' worry, babes and all.
    I s'pose things go by some big rule
Of God's own book, but my ol' brain
    Can't fix 'um up, so I'll just wait
An' do my duty when it's clear,
    An' trust to Him to make it straight.
— Goodness! noon is almost here,
    And there the men come through the gate!

THE SOCIABLE AT DUDLEY'S

THE SOCIABLE AT DUDLEY'S

I

JOHN JENNINGS was not one of those men who go to a donation party with fifty cents' worth of potatoes and eat and carry away two dollars' worth of turkey and jelly-cake. When he drove his team around to the front door for Mrs. Jennings, he had a sack of flour and a quarter of a fine fat beef in his sleigh and a five-dollar bill in his pocket-book, a contribution to Elder Wheat's support.

Milton, his twenty-year-old son, was just driving out of the yard, seated in a fine new cutter, drawn by a magnificent young gray horse. He drew up as Mr. Jennings spoke.

"Now be sure and don't never leave him a minute untied; and see that the harness is all right. Do you hear, Milton?"

"Yes, I hear!" answered the young fellow, rather impatiently, for he thought himself old enough and big enough to look out for himself.

"Don't race, will y', Milton?" was his mother's anxious question from the depth of her shawls.

"Not if I can help it," was his equivocal response as he chirruped to Marc Antony. The grand brute made a rearing leap that brought a cry from the mother and a

laugh from the young driver, and swung into the road at
a flying pace. The night was clear and cold, the sleigh-
ing excellent, and the boy's heart was full of exultation.

It was a joy just to control such a horse as he drew
rein over that night. Large, with the long, lithe body
of a tiger and the broad, clear limbs of an elk, the gray
colt strode away up the road, his hoofs flinging a shower
of snow over the dasher. The lines were like steel
rods; the sleigh literally swung by them; the traces
hung slack inside the thills. The bell clashed out a
swift clamor; the runners seemed to hiss over the snow
as the duck-breasted cutter swung round the curves, and
softly rose and fell along the undulating road.

On either hand the snow stood billowed against the
fences and amid the wide fields of corn-stalks bleached
in the wind. Over in the east, above the line of timber
skirting Cedar Creek, the vast, slightly gibbous moon
was rising, sending along the crusted snow a broad path
of light. Other sleighs could be heard through the still,
cold air. Far away a party of four or five were singing
a chorus as they spun along the road.

Something sweet and unnamable was stirring in the
young fellow's brain as he spun along in the marvellously
still and radiant night. He wished Eileen were with
him. The vast and cloudless blue vault of sky glittered
with stars, which even the radiant moon could not dim.
Not a breath of air was stirring save that made by the
swift, strong stride of the horse.

It was a night for youth and love and bells, and Milton felt this consciously, and felt it by singing : —

"Stars of the summer night,
    Hide in your azure deeps, —
    She sleeps — my lady sleeps."

He was on his way to get Bettie Moss, one of his old sweethearts, who had become more deeply concerned with the life of Edwin Blackler. He had taken the matter with sunny philosophy, even before meeting Eileen Deering at the Seminary, and he was now on his way to bring about peace between Ed and Bettie, who had lately quarrelled. Incidentally he expected to enjoy the sleigh-ride.

"Stiddy, boy! Ho, boy! *Stiddy*, old fellow," he called soothingly to Marc, as he neared the gate and whirled up to the door. A girl came to the door as he drove up, her head wrapped in a white hood, a shawl on her arms. She had been waiting for him.

"Hello, Milt. That you?"

"It's me. Been waiting?"

"I should say I had. Begun t' think you'd gone back on me. Everybody else's gone."

"Well! Hop in here before you freeze; we'll not be the last ones there. Yes, bring the shawl; you'll need it t' keep the snow off your face," he called authoritatively.

"'Tain't snowin', is it?" she asked as she shut the door and came to the sleigh's side.

"Clear as a bell," he said as he helped her in.

"Then where'll the snow come from?"

"From Marc's heels."

"Goodness sakes! you don't expect me t' ride after *that* wild-headed critter, do you?"

His answer was a chirp which sent Marc halfway to the gate before Bettie could catch her breath. The reins stiffened in his hands. Bettie clung to him, shrieking at every turn in the road.

"Milton Jennings, if you tip us over, I'll—"

Milton laughed, drew the colt down to a steady, swift stride, and Bettie put her hands back under the robe.

"I wonder who that is ahead?" he asked after a few minutes, which brought them in sound of bells.

"I guess it's Cy Hurd; it sounded like his bells when he went past. I guess it's him and Bill an' Belle an' Cad Hines."

"Expect to see Ed there?" asked Milton, after a little pause.

"I don't care whether I ever see him again or not," she snapped.

"Oh, yes, you do!" he answered, feeling somehow her insincerity.

"Well—I don't!"

Milton didn't care to push the peace-making any further. However, he had curiosity enough to ask, "What upset things 'tween you 'n Ed?"

"Oh, nothing."

"You mean none o' my business?"

"I didn't say so."

"No, you didn't need to," he laughed, and she joined in.

"Yes, that's Cy Hurd. I know that laugh of his

far's I c'n hear it," said Bettie as they jingled along. "I wonder who's with him?"

"We'll mighty soon see," said Milton, as he wound the lines around his hands and braced his feet, giving a low whistle, which seemed to run through the colt's blood like fire. His stride did not increase in rate, but its reach grew majestic as he seemed to lengthen and lower. His broad feet flung great disks of hard-packed snow over the dasher, and under the clash of his bells the noise of the other team grew plainer.

"Get out of the way," sang Milton, as he approached the other team. There was challenge and exultation in his tone.

"Hello! In a hurry?" shouted those in front, without increasing their own pace.

"Ya-as, something of a hurry," drawled Milton in a disguised voice.

"Wa-al? Turn out an' go by if you are."

"No, thankee, I'll just let m' nag nibble the hay out o' your box an' take it easy."

"Sure o' that?"

"You bet high I am." Milton nudged Bettie, who was laughing with delight. "It's Bill an' his bays. He thinks there isn't a team in the country can keep up with him. "Get out o' the way there!" he shouted again. "I'm in a hurry."

"Let 'em out, let 'em out, Bill," they heard Cy say, and the bays sprang forward along the level road, the bells ringing like mad, the snow flying, the girls scream-ing at every lurch of the sleighs. But Marc's head still shook haughtily above the end gate; still the foam from his lips fell upon the hay in the box ahead.

"Git out o' this! Yip!" yelled Bill to his bays, but Marc merely made a lunging leap and tugged at the lines as if asking for more liberty. Milton gave him his head, and laughed to see the great limbs rise and fall like the pistons of an engine. They swept over the weeds like a hawk skimming the stubble of a wheat-field.

"Git out o' the way or I'll run right over your back," yelled Milton again.

"Try it," was the reply.

"Grab hold of me, Bettie, and lean to the right. When we turn this corner I'm going to take the inside track and pass 'em."

"You'll tip us over —"

"No, I won't! Do as I tell you."

They were nearing a wide corner, where the road turned to the right and bore due south through the woods. Milton caught sight of the turn, gave a quick twist of the lines around his hands, leaned over the dasher and spoke shrilly: —

"Git out o' this, Marc!"

The splendid brute swerved to the right, and made a leap that seemed to lift the sleigh and all into the air. The snow flew in such stinging showers Milton could see nothing. The sleigh was on one runner, heeling like a yacht in a gale; the girl was clinging to his neck; he could hear the bells of the other sleigh to his left; Marc was passing them; he heard shouts and the swish of a whip. Another convulsive effort of the gray, and then Milton found himself in the road again, in the moonlight, where the apparently unwearied horse, with head out-thrust, nostril wide-blown, and body squared, was trotting like a veteran on the track. The team was behind.

"Stiddy, boy!"

Milton soothed Marc down to a long, easy pace; then turned to Bettie, who had uncovered her face again.

"How d' y' like it?"

"My sakes! I don't want any more of that. If I'd 'a' known you was goin' t' drive like that I wouldn't 'a' come. You're worse'n Ed. I expected every minute we'd be down in the ditch. But, oh! ain't he jest splendid?" she added, in admiration of the horse.

"Don't y' want to drive him?"

"Oh, yes; let me try. I drive our teams."

She took the lines, and at Milton's suggestion wound them around her hands. She looked very pretty with the moon shining on her face, her eyes big and black with excitement, and Milton immediately put his arm around her, and laid his head on her shoulder.

"Milton Jennings, if you don't —"

"Look out," he cried in mock alarm, "don't you drop those lines!" He gave her a severe hug.

"Milton Jennings, you let go me!"

"That's what you said before."

"Take these lines."

"Can't do it," he laughed; "my hands are cold. Got to warm them, see?" He pulled off his mitten and put his icy hand under her chin. The horse was going at a tremendous pace again.

" O-o-o-oh ! If you don't take these lines I'll drop 'em, so there ! "

" Don't y' do it," he called warningly ; but she did, and boxed his ears soundly while he was getting Marc in hand again. Bettie's rage was fleeting as the blown breath from Marc's nostrils, and when Milton turned to her again all was as if his deportment had been grave and cavalier.

The stinging air made itself felt, and they drew close under their huge buffalo robes as Marc strode steadily forward. The dark groves fell behind, the clashing bells marked the rods and miles, and kept time to the songs they hummed.

> " Jingle, bells ! Jingle, bells !
> Jingle all the way.
> Oh, what joy it is to ride
> In a one-horse open sleigh."

They overtook another laughing, singing load of young folks — a great wood sleigh packed full with boys and girls, two and two — hooded girls, and boys with caps drawn down over their ears. A babel of tongues arose from the sweeping, creaking bob-sleigh, and rose into the silent air like a mighty peal of laughter.

II

A SCHOOLHOUSE set beneath the shelter of great oaks was the centre of motion and sound. On one side of it the teams stood shaking their bells under their insufficient blankets, making a soft chorus of fitful trills heard in the pauses of the merry shrieks of the boys playing "pom-pom pull-away" across the road before the house, which radiated light and laughter. A group of young men stood on the porch as Milton drove up.

"Hello, Milt," said a familiar voice as he reined Marc close to the step.

"That you, Shep?"

"Chuss, it's me," replied Shep.

"How'd you know me so far off?"

"Puh! Don't y' s'pose I know that horse an' those bells — Miss Moss, allow me — " He helped her out with elaborate courtesy. "The supper and the old folks are *here*, and the girls and boys and the fun is over to Dudley's," he explained as he helped Bettie out.

"I'll be back soon's I put my horse up," said Milton to Bettie. "You go in and get good 'n' warm, and then we'll go over to the house."

"I saved a place in the barn for you, Milt. I knew you'd never let Marc stand out in the snow," said Shephard as he sprang in beside Milton.

"I knew you would. What's the news? Is Ed here t'night?"

"Yeh-up. On deck with S'fye Kinney. It'll make him *swear* when he finds out who Bettie come with."

"Let him. Are the Yohe boys here?"

"Yep. They're alwiss on hand, like a sore thumb. Bill's been drinking, and is likely to give Ed trouble.

He never'll give Bettie up without a fight.   Look out
he don't jump onto *your* neck."

" No danger o' that," said Milton, coolly.

The Yohe boys were strangers in the neighborhood.
They had come in with the wave of harvest help from
the South and had stayed on into the winter, making
few friends and a large number of enemies among the
young men of the Grove.   Everybody admitted that
they had metal in them, for they instantly paid court to
the prettiest girls in the neighborhood without regard to
any prior claims.

And the girls were attracted by these Missourians,
their air of mysterious wickedness, and their muscular
swagger, precisely as a flock of barn-yard fowl are interested in the strange bird thrust among them.

But the Southerners had muscles like wildcats, and
their feats of broil and battle commanded a certain re-
spectful consideration.   In fact, most of the young men
of the district were afraid of the red-faced, bold-eyed
strangers, one of the few exceptions being Milton, and
another Shephard Watson, his friend and room-mate at
the Rock River Seminary.   Neither of these boys being
at all athletic, it was rather curious that Bill and Joe
Yohe should treat them with so much consideration.

Bill was standing before the huge cannon stove, talking with Bettie, when Milton and Shephard returned to
the schoolhouse.   The man's hard black eyes were
filled with a baleful fire, and his wolfish teeth shone
through his long red mustache.   It made Milton mutter
under his breath to see how innocently Bettie laughed

with him.   She never dreamed, and could not have com-
prehended, the vileness of the man's whole life and
thought.   No lizard revelled in the mud more hideously
than he.   His conversation reeked with obscenity.   His
tongue dropped poison each moment when among his
own sex, and his eyes blazed it forth when in the
presence of women.

"Hello, Bill," said Milton, with easy indifference.
"How goes it?"

"Oh, 'bout so-so   You rather got ahead o' me
t'night, didn't yeh?"

"Well, rather.   The man that gets ahead o' me has
got t' drive a good team, eh?"   He looked at Bettie.

"I'd like to try it," said Bill.

"Well, let's go across the road," said Milton to
Bettie, anxious to get her out of the way of Bill.

They had to run the gauntlet of the whooping boys
outside, but Bettie proved too fleet of foot for them all.

When they entered the Dudley house opposite, her
cheeks were hot with color, but the roguish gleam in
her eyes changed to a curiously haughty and disdainful
look as she passed Blackler, who stood desolately beside
the door, looking awkward and sullen.

Milton was a great favorite, and had no time to say
anything more to Bettie as peace-maker.   He reached
Ed as soon as possible.

"Ed, what's up between you and Bettie?"

"Oh, I don't know.   I can't find out," Blackler replied, and he spurred himself desperately into the fun.

III

"It'll make Ed Blackler squirm t' see Betsey come in on Milt Jennings's arm," said Bill to Shephard after Milton went out.

"Wal, chuss. I denk it will." Shephard was looking round the room, where the old people were noisily eating supper, and the steaming oysters and the cold chicken's savory smell went to his heart. One of the motherly managers of the feast bustled up to him.

"Shephard, you run over t' the house an' tell the young folks that they can come over t' supper about eight o'clock; that'll be in a half an hour. You understand?"

"Oh, I'm so hungry! Can't y' give me a hunk o' chicken t' stay m' stomach?"

Mrs. Councill laughed. "I'll fish you out a drumstick," she said. And he went away, gnawing upon it hungrily. Bill went with him, still belching forth against Blackler.

"Jim said he heard *he* said he'd slap my face f'r a cent. I wish he would. I'd lick the life out of 'im in a minnit."

"Why don't you pitch into Milt? He's got her now. He's the one y'd orto be dammin'."

"Oh, he don't mean nothin' by it. He don't care for her. I saw him down to town at the show with the girl he's after. He's jest makin' Ed mad."

A game of "Copenhagen" was going on as they entered. Bettie was in the midst of it, but Milton, in the corner, was looking on and talking with a group of those who had outgrown such games.

The ring of noisy, flushed, and laughter-intoxicated young people filled the room nearly to the wall, and round and round the ring flew Bettie, pursued by Joe Yohe.

"Go it, Joe!" yelled Bill.

"You're good f'r 'im," yelled Shephard.

Milton laughed and clapped his hands. "Hot foot, Bettie!"

Like another Atalanta, the superb young girl sped, now dodging through the ring, now doubling as her pursuer tried to catch her by turning back. At last she made the third circuit, and, breathless and laughing, took her place in the line. But Joe rushed upon her, determined to steal a kiss anyhow.

"H'yare! H'yare! None o' that."

"That's no fair," cried the rest, and he was caught by a dozen hands.

"She didn't go round three times," he said.

"Yes, she did," cried a dozen voices.

"You shut up," he retorted brutally, looking at Ed Blackler, who had not spoken at all. Ed glared back, but said nothing. Bettie ignored Ed, and the game went on.

"There's going to be trouble here to-night," said Milton to Shephard.

Shephard, as the ring dissolved, stepped into the middle of the room and flourished his chicken-leg as if it were a baton. After the burst of laughter, his sonorous voice made itself heard.

" Come to supper! Everybody take his girl if he can, and if he can't — get the other feller's girl."

Bill Yohe sprang toward Bettie, but Milton had touched her on the arm.

" Not t'night, Bill," he smilingly said.

Bill grinned in reply and made off toward another well-known belle, Ella Pratt, who accepted his escort. Ed Blackler, with gloomy desperation, took Maud Peters, the most depressingly plain girl in the room, an action which did not escape Bettie's eyes, and which softened her heart toward him; but she did not let·him see it.

Supper was served on the desks, each couple seated in the drab-colored wooden seats as if they were at school. A very comfortable arrangement for those who occupied the back seats, but torture to the adults who were obliged to cramp their legs inside the desk where the primer class sat on school-days.

Bettie saw with tenderness how devotedly poor Ed served Maud. He could not have taken a better method of heaping coals of fire on her head.

Ed was entirely unconscious of her softening, however, for he could not look around from where he sat. He heard her laughing and believed she was happy. He had not taken poor Maud for the purpose of showing his penitence, for he had no such feeling in his heart; he was, on the contrary, rather gloomy and reckless. He was not in a mood to show a front of indifference.

The oysters steamed; the heels of the boys' boots thumped in wild delight; the women bustled about;

the girls giggled, and the men roared with laughter. Everybody ate as if he and she had never tasted oyster-soup and chicken before, and the cakes and pies went the way of the oyster-soup like corn before a troop of winter turkeys.

Bill Yohe, by way of a joke, put some frosting down Cy Hurd's back, and, by way of delicate attention to Ella, alternately shoved her out of the seat and pulled her back again, while Joe hurled a chicken-leg at Cad Hines as she stood in the entry-way. Will Kinney told Sary Hines for the fourth time how his team had run away, interrupted by his fear that some kind of pie would get away untasted.

"An' so I laid the lines down — H'yare! Gimme another handful of crackers, Merry, — an' I laid the lines down while I went t' find — Nary a noyster I can hold any more. Mrs. Moss, I'm ready f'r pie now — an' so I noticed ole Frank's eye kind o' roll, but thinksi, I c'n git holt o' the lines if he — Yes'm, I alwiss eat mince; won't you try some, Sary? — an' — an' — so, jest as I gut my axe — You bet! I'm goin' t' try a piece of every kind if it busts my stummick. Gutta git my money's worth."

Milton was in his best mood and was very attractive in his mirth. His fine teeth shone and his yellow curls shook under the stress of his laughter. He wrestled with Bettie for the choice bits of cake, delighting in the touch of her firm, sweet flesh; and, as for Bettie, she was almost charmed to oblivion of Ed by the superior attractions of Milton's town-bred manners. Ed looked singu-

T

larly awkward and lonesome as he sat sprawled out in one of the low seats, and curiously enough his uncouthness and disconsolateness of attitude won her heart back again.

Everybody, with the usual rustic freedom, had remarks to make upon the situation.

"Wal, Bettie, made a swop, hev yeh?" said Councill.

"Hello, Milt; thought you had a girl down town."

"Oh, I keep one at each end of the line," said Milton, with his ready laugh.

"Wal, I swan t' gudgeon! I can't keep track o' you town fellers. You're too many f'r me!" said Mrs. Councill.

Carrie Hines came up behind Milton and Bettie and put her arms around their necks, bringing their cheeks together. Bettie grew purple with anger and embarrassment, but Milton, with his usual readiness, said, "Thank you," and reached for the tittering malefactor's waist. Nobody noticed it, for the room was full of such romping.

The men were standing around the stove discussing political outlooks, and the matrons were busy with the serving of the supper. Out of doors the indefatigable boys were beginning again on "pom-pom pull-away."

Supper over, the young folks all returned to the house across the way, leaving the men of elderly blood to talk on the Grange and the uselessness of the middlemen. Sport began again in the Dudley farmhouse by a dozen or so of the young people "forming on" for "Weevily Wheat."

"Weevily Wheat" was a "donation dance." As it

would have been wicked to have a fiddle to play the music, singers were substituted with stirring effect, and a song was sung, while the couples bowed and balanced and swung in rhythm to it : —

> "Come *hither*, my love, and *trip* together
>   In the morning early,
> I'll give to *you* the parting hand,
>   Although I love you dearly.
> But I *won't* have none of y'r weevily wheat,
>   An' I *won't* have *none* of y'r barley,
> But I'll have some flour in a half an hour
>   To bake a cake for Charley.

> "Oh, Charley, *he* is a fine young man ;
>   Charley, he is a dandy.
> Oh, Charley, *he's* a fine young man,
>   F'r he buys the girls some candy.
> Oh, I *won't* have none o' y'r weevily wheat,
>   I won't have *none* o' y'r barley,
> But I'll have some flour in a half an hour
>   To bake a cake for Charley.

> "Oh, Charley, he's," etc.

Milton was soon in the thick of this most charming old-fashioned dance, which probably dates back to dances on the green in England or Norway. Bettie was a good dancer, and as she grew excited with the rhythm and swing of the quaint, plaintive music, her form grew supple at the waist and her large limbs light.   The pair moved up and back between the two ranks of singers, then down the outside, and laughed in glee when they accelerated the pace at the time when they were swinging down the centre. All faces were aglow and eyes shining.

Bill's red face and bullet eyes were not beautiful, but the grace and power of his body were unmistakable. He was excited by the music, the alcohol he had been drinking, and by the presence of the girls, and threw himself into the play with dangerous abandon.

Under his ill-fitting coat his muscles rolled swift and silent. His tall boots were brilliantly blue and starred with gold at the top, and his pantaloons were tucked inside the tops to let their glory strike the eye. His physical strength and grace and variety of " steps " called forth many smiles and admiring exclamations from the girls, and caused the young men to lose interest in " Weevily Wheat."

When a new set was called for, Bill made a determined assault on Bettie and secured her, for she did not have the firmness to refuse. But the singers grew weary, and the set soon broke up. A game of forfeits was substituted. This also dwindled down to a mere excuse for lovers to kiss each other, and the whole company soon separated into little groups to chatter and romp. Some few sat at the table in the parlor and played " authors."

Bettie was becoming annoyed by the attentions of Bill, and, to get rid of him, went with Miss Lytle, Milton, and two or three others into another room and shut the door. This was not very unusual, but poor Blackler seemed to feel it a direct affront to him and was embittered. He was sitting by Ella Pratt when Bill Yohe swaggered up to him.

"Say! Do you know where your girl is?"

"No, an' I don't care."

"Wal! It's *time* y' cared. She's in the other room there. Milt Jennings has cut you out."

"You're a liar," cried the loyal lover, leaping to his feet.

Spat! Yohe's open palm resounded upon the pale face of Blackler, whose eyes had a wild glare in them, and the next moment they were rolling on the floor like a couple of dogs, the stronger and older man above, the valiant lover below. The house resounded with sudden screams, a hurry of feet followed, then a hush, in the midst of which was heard the unsubdued voice of Blackler as he rose to his feet.

"You're a —"

Another dull stroke with the knotted fist, and the young fellow went to the floor again, while Joe Yohe, like a wild beast roused at the sight of blood, stood above the form of his brother (who had leaped upon the fallen man), shouting with the hoarse, raucous note of a tiger : —

"Give 'im hell! I'll back yeh."

Bettie pushed through the ring of men and women who were looking on in delicious horror — pushed through quickly and yet with dignity. Her head was thrown back, and the strange look on her face was thrilling. Facing the angry men with a gesture of superb scorn and fearlessness, she spoke, and in the deep hush her quiet words were strangely impressive : —

"Bill Yohe, what do you think you're doing?"

For a moment the men were abashed, and, starting back, they allowed Blackler, dazed, bleeding, and half strangled, to rise to his feet. He would have sprung against them both, for he had not heard or realized who was speaking, but Bettie laid her hand on his arm, and the haughty droop of her eyelids changed as she said in a tender voice : —

"Never mind, Ed; they ain't worth mindin'!"

Her usual self came back quickly as she led him away. Friends began to mutter now, and the swagger of the brothers threatened further trouble. Their eyes rolled, their knotted hands swung about like bludgeons. Threats, horrible snarls, and oaths poured from their lips. But there were heard at this critical moment rapid footsteps — a round, jovial voice — and bursting through the door came the great form and golden head of Lime Gilman.

"Hold on here! What's all this?" he said, leaping with an ominously good-natured smile into the open space before the two men, whose restless pacing stopped at the sound of his voice. His sunny, laughing blue eyes swept around him, taking in the situation at a glance. He continued to smile, but his teeth came together.

"Git out o' this, you hounds! Git!" he said, in the same jovial tone. "You! *You*," he said to Bill, slapping him lightly on the breast with the back of his lax fingers. Bill struck at him ferociously, but the slope-shouldered giant sent it by with his left wrist, kicking the feet of the striker from under him with a frightful swing of his right foot, — a trick which appalled Joe.

" Clear the track there," ordered Lime. " It's against the law t' fight at a donation ; so out y' go."

Bill crawled painfully to his feet.

" I'll pay you for this yet."

" *Any* time but now. Git out, 'r I'll kick you out." Lime's voice changed now. The silent crowd made way for them, and, seizing Joe by the shoulder and pushing Bill before him, the giant passed out into the open air. There he pushed Bill off the porch into the snow, and kicked his brother over him with this parting word : —

" You infernal hyenies ! Kickin's too good f'r you. If you ever want me, look around an' you'll find me."

Then, to the spectators who thronged after, he apologized : —

" I hate t' fight, and especially to kick a man ; but they's times when a man's *got* t' do it. Now, jest go back and have a good time. Don't let them hyenies spoil all y'r fun."

That ended it. All knew Lime. Everybody had heard that he could lift one end of a separator and toss a two-bushel sack filled with wheat over the hind wheel of a wagon, and the terror of his kick was not unknown to them. They were certain the Yohes would not return, and all went back into the house and attempted to go on with the games. But it was impossible ; such exciting events must be discussed, and the story was told and retold by each one.

When Milton returned to the parlor, he saw Bettie,

tender, dignified, and grave, bending over Blackler, bathing his bruised face. Milton had never admired her more than at that moment; she looked so womanly. She no longer cared what people thought.

The other girls, pale and tearful and a little hysterical, stood about, close to their sweethearts. They enjoyed the excitement, however, and the fight appealed to something organic in them.

The donation party was at an end, that was clear, and the people began to get ready to go home. Bettie started to thank Lyman for his help.

"Don't say anything. I'd 'a' done it jest the same f'r anybody. It ain't the thing to come to a donation and git up a row."

Milton hardly knew whether to ask Bettie to go back with him or not, but Blackler relieved him from embarrassment by rousing up and saying : —

"Oh, I'm all right now, Bettie. Hyere's yer girl, Milt. See the eye I've got on me? She says she won't ride home with any such — "

"Ed, what in the world do you mean?" Bettie could hardly understand her lover's sudden exultation; it was still a very serious matter to her, in spite of the complete reconciliation which had come with the assault. She felt in a degree guilty, and that feeling kept her still tearful and subdued, but Ed leered and winked with his good eye in uncontrollable delight. Milton turned to Bettie at last, and said : —

"Well! I'll get Marc around to the door in a few minutes. Get your things on."

Bettie and Ed stood close together by the door. She
was saying : —

"You'll forgive me, won't you, Ed?"

"Why, course I will, Bettie. I was as much to blame
as you was. I no business to git mad till I knew what
I was gittin' mad *at*."

They were very tender now.

"I'll—I'll go home with you, if you want me to,
'stead of with Milt," she quavered.

"No, I've got to take S'fye home. It's the square
thing."

"All right, Ed, but come an' let me talk it all
straight."

"It's all straight now; let's let it all go, what do
you say?"

"All right, Ed."

There was a kiss which the rest pretended not to
hear, and bidding them all good night, Bettie ran out
to the fence, where Milton sat waiting.

The moon was riding high in the clear, cold sky, but
falling toward the west, as they swung into the wood
road. Through the branches of the oaks the stars, set
in the deep-blue, fathomless night, peered cold and
bright. There was no wind save the rush of air caused
by the motion of the sleigh. Neither of the young
people spoke for some time. They lay back in the
sleigh under the thick robes, listening to the chime of
the bells, the squeal of the runners, and the weirdly
sweet distant singing of another sleigh-load of young
people far ahead.

Milton pulled Marc down to a slow trot, and, tightening his arm around Bettie's shoulders in a very brotherly hug, said : —

"Well, I'm glad you and Ed have fixed things up again. You'd always have been sorry."

"It was all my fault, anyway," replied the girl, with a little tremor in her voice, "and it was all my fault to-night, too. I no business to 'a' gone off an' left him that way."

"Well, it's all over now, anyway, and so I wouldn't worry any more about it," said Milton, soothingly, and then they fell into silence again.

The sagacious Marc Antony strode steadily away, and the two young lovers went on with their dreaming. Bettie was silent mainly, and Milton, his mind filled with love for Eileen, was remembering the long rides they had had together. And the horse's hoofs beat a steady rhythm, the moon fell to the west, and the bells kept cheery chime. The breath of the horse rose into the air like steam. The house-dogs sent forth warning howls as they went by. Once or twice they passed houses where the windows were still lighted and where lanterns were flashing around the barn, where the horses were being put in for the night.

The lights were out at the home of Bettie when they drove up, for the young people, however rapidly they might go to the sociable, always returned much slower than the old folks. Milton leaped out and held up his arms to help his companion down. As she shook the robes free, stood up and reached out for his arms, he seized her round the waist, and, holding her clear of the ground, kissed her in spite of her struggles.

"Milton!"

"The last time, Bettie; the last time," he said, in extenuation. With this mournful word on his lips he leaped into the sleigh and was off like the wind. But the listening girl heard his merry voice ringing out on the still air. Suddenly something sweet and majestic swept upon her — something which made her look up into the glittering sky with vast yearning. In the awful hush of the sky and the plain she heard the beat of her own blood in her ears. She longed for song to express the swelling of her throat and the wistful ache of her heart.

AN AFTERWORD: OF WINDS,
SNOWS, AND THE STARS. . . . . .

O witchery of the winter night
  (With broad moon shouldering to the west)!

In the city streets the west wind sweeps
Before my feet in rustling flight;
The midnight snows in untracked heaps
Lie cold and desolate and white.
I stand and wait with upturned eyes,
Awed with the splendor of the skies
And star-trained progress of the moon.

The city walls dissolve like smoke
Beneath the magic of the moon,
And age falls from me like a cloak;
I hear sweet girlish voices ring
Clear as some softly stricken string —
(The moon is sailing to the west.)
The sleigh-bells clash in homeward flight;
With frost each horse's breast is white —
(The big moon sinking to the west.)
        *   *   *   *   *
    " Good night, Lettie !"
    " Good night, Ben !"
(The moon is sinking at the west.)
" Good night, my sweetheart."   Once again
The parting kiss while comrades wait
Impatient at the roadside gate,
And the red moon sinks beyond the west.